TRIALS

of the

FOUR

OLYMPIANS

TRIALS

of the

FOUR

OLYMPIANS

Rebecca J. Sotirios

Rev. date: 04/28/2021

To order additional copies of this book, contact:
Xlibris
AU TFN: 1 800 844 927 (Toll Free inside Australia)
AU Local: 0283 108 187 (+61 2 8310 8187 from outside Australia)
www.Xlibris.com.au
Orders@Xlibris.com.au
825384

CONTENTS

To my dad, who assisted me on this fantastic journey to write my first novel, and to my mother, who made me do something productive.

Dear Mortal,

If you have found this book, please read with caution. Everything that takes place in this Novel is true. It's based on the fates of four demigods.

But I must warn you. There are evil forces out there that do not wish for you to read this. They will do anything in their power to prevent you from knowing the truth.

Be careful and act like your every move is being watched . . .
Because it very well might be.
Stay Safe.

Iris Dimitriadis.

MEET THE CHARACTERS

Name: Iris Dimitriadis
Age: 18
Parent: Unknown

Name: Alexandros Papatonis
Age: 20
Parent: Hades

**Name: Anastasia (Tia)
Papathanasiou**
Age: 18
Parent: Poseidon

Name: Theodore (Theo) Drakos
Age: 19
Parent: Apollo

CHAPTER 1

⟨⟩

The Beginning

In the beginning, there was nothing, a lot of nothing. There is no way to possibly know how the world was created.

But I am going to tell you the creation story that the Ancient Greeks believed.

But I warn you… It is not pleasant.

From the genesis, the world was in a state of nothingness, called Chaos, drifting around in the cosmos. Chaos was soon joined by three other deities that appeared out of a formless void: Gaia (earth), Tartarus (underworld), and Eros (love).

Gaia and Eros formed together to create every known and unknown thing throughout the universe. Birthing twelve Titans to roam the Earth, but one well-known Titan became the soul existence of the Olympian gods.

His name was Cronus. He became the ruler of earth, marrying his sister Rhea, who bore him five children.

But Cronus, being afraid of a prophecy that he had received from Gaia, that he would soon be overthrown by one of his sons, resulted in him eating his own children.

He definitely won the 'Best Father in the Galaxy' award.

Rhea, realising she was with child, her sixth son, decided to give birth to him in a far-off island, Crete, and raised him there with the nymphs. This child was named Zeus.

After being raised by the nymphs, Zeus disguised himself as a servant in his father's realm, chose to poison his father's drink, which resulted in Cronus throwing up his children: Hera, Hades, Poseidon, Demeter, and Hestia. The children, being immortal, had been growing up completely undigested in Cronus's stomach.

The gods revolted against their father and defeated him. Zeus won with the help of the cyclops. After the war, Zeus cut Cronus into pieces and threw him into the depths of Tartarus, down in the underworld, leaving Zeus to reign over Mount Olympus with his godly siblings.

Zeus became the god of the sky, Hera the goddess of marriage, Poseidon the god of the sea, Demeter the goddess of agriculture, and Hades the god of the underworld.

Trust me, I know what you are thinking . . . This sounds like a *whole* load of nonsense.

You might not believe in them… but they are out there, and their very own offspring may be living amongst you.

Before I get too carried away with the story, let me just fill you in on some small crucial details.

When a god has a child with a mortal, the result is a demigod.

And that is what I am.

Careful, you may very well have heard about us in ancient legends: Achilles, Hercules, Theseus, and Per*seus*. There is a lot of us out there. *I will stop myself before I get carried away.*

Most demigods only meet their godly parents when they receive a prophecy. I, on the other hand, have not received one, so I haven't the slightest clue who my father is.

The only positive side about being a child of a god is that we have above-average strength, knowledge, and charisma. We know Ancient and Modern Greek extremely well, but only the strongest of us have control over the realm our godly parent rules over.

All right, enough of that, now let me tell you the story of four demigods that were destined to save Olympus.

My name is Iris Dimitriadis, and today is my eighteenth birthday. Something weird just happened recently, and am I one of these demigods living amongst you? As a young Greek, I was encouraged to visit the oracle of Delphi.

CHAPTER 2

The Prophecy

A t the age of eighteen, each demigod is sent to visit the oracle of Delphi but never during the day. The best time to visit the oracle would be at sunset, when no tourists are around to see anything out of the norm.

I didn't believe in the Greek gods, I always thought they were myths, or stories parents would tell to scare their misbehaving children back into line.

The whole ordeal of someone-something out there, so much bigger than me, really puts things into perspective.

I can still recall the conversation I had with my Aunt about this, like it was only yesterday. I had a right to find out the truth about myself; I'd rather be safe than sorry.

The Oracle of Delphi will either give me good news or the news my family and I have been dreading to find out. That I'm one of those . . . those demigods. The ones the gods would terrorize for the fun of it.

Weird occurrences have been happening to me since I turned sixteen years old, the weather would change depending on the mood I was in. Birds or should I say eagles, become attracted to me, following me, keeping a close eye on me, whenever I would stray too far from home. What was even more unique, was that I could feel their emotions, a spiritual connection towards them, like they had a greater meaning or purpose.

With every bone in my body crossed, I really hope these bizarre occurrences are nothing other than that, just bizarre.

That's why I'm visiting the Oracle of Delphi, her prophecies will answer everything that's unanswered.

You're probably asking, 'what's a prophecy?'

A prophecy is a prediction of events that will take place in the future. There are many ways for a prophecy to be told, but the one the Greeks used most was from an Oracle, the Oracle of Delphi.

In Ancient Greece, people would travel from around the world, just to have heard the words of the Oracle, who would speak the words of Apollo-the god of prophecies.

Delphi was known as one of the most sacred places in Ancient Greece. The city of Delphi thrived in Ancient Greece. Now, it has become an archeology site, filled with everyday tourists.

I arrive at the site of Delphi as soon as the sun began to set, the night air was fresh, but the heat of the summer day was still present as I make my way to where the oracle of Delphi was said to be. I watch my footing as I step over rocks and loose gravel, slowly making my way to the fore temple of Delphi. As I reach the ancient steps that lead to the temple, everything goes silent, including the birds chirping in the trees. Off in the distance, I see a couple of nymphs watching in awe as I make my way up the fragile stone steps, none of them daring to look away, just in case they miss what's about to take place.

The mist covering the temple from everyday tourists begins to fade away as I reach the top of the stairs, being replaced with the real temple of Delphi. I take in the temple in front of me, tall white marble columns holding up the temple's roof.

'Hello?' I whisper into the night air, hoping to receive an answer.

Moments pass, as I receive no reply. The temple is completely empty, with only a lonely concrete square slab that rises a few metres of the ground, a small hole engraved in the middle. Unlit torches hang off the marble columns. I carefully make my way towards the slab, crouching down beside the monument, so that my face is level with the hole. This time, instead of speaking, I place a few drachmas inside the gap. It has been told that if you wish to summon the spirit of Delphi, one has to offer a sacrifice. However, in modern days, just a few drachmas will do the trick.

As soon as the drachmas are placed, they disappear into green mist. In front of me, a spirit slowly takes form of a middle-aged female on the other side of the concrete slab. The unlit torches around the temple suddenly light up in green flames. I stumble backwards, startled. The woman standing in front of me has a dark aura around her, green mists replace her eyes. She looks directly at me, as if she is looking straight through me.

'I am the spirit of Delphi, the Oracle of Apollo, speaking the prophecy of the Olympian gods. Approach, demigod, and ask,' says the oracle in a deep, emotionless voice, sending a chill down my spine.

"I . . . I . . . " I was lost for words.

Come on! Snap out of it. I know what I am here for, put your big-girl pants on, and ask.

'I . . . have just reached the age of eighteen, and I haven't been claimed by my godly parent.' I pause again before adding, 'May I know who he is?'

Silence fills the temple, but all I can hear is my heart pounding in my chest.

'Knowing yourself is the beginning of all wisdom. Your father is the god of the beginning and the end,' says the oracle.

'Zeus....' I whisper in disbelief. Zeus is my father, god of the sky, the king of Mount Olympus.

As if ignoring my response, the oracle continues, 'When rain falls in cloudless skies, Olympus will be known once more. I warn you, the souls of the dead and the living will see no peace until Olympus is saved or razed to the ground. Four demigods, the offspring of each of the gods Zeus, Poseidon, Hades, and Apollo, none older than the age of twenty-five, will either bring chaos or raise Mount Olympus from the hold of evil.'

And with that, she disappears, extinguishing the torches around the temple whilst doing so, leaving me in complete darkness. As I stand there in silence, her words replay in my head. Oh no . . . I start to panic, my heart beating faster than ever. I had just received a prophecy.

CHAPTER 3

Joining The Party

Receiving a prophecy as a demigod rarely turns out to be a positive thing; most of the time it sends us to our deaths.

Standing within the now-empty walls of Delphi, the haunting words of the oracle repeat in my head as I try to make sense of it all.

'When rain falls in cloudless skies, Olympus will be known once more. I warn you, the souls of the dead and the living will see no peace until Olympus is saved or razed to the ground. Four demigods, the offspring of each of the gods Zeus, Poseidon, Hades, and Apollo, none older than the age of twenty-five, will either bring chaos or raise Mount Olympus from the hold of evil.'

A bright light appears in front of me, squinting my eyes shut, as I use my free hand to shield my eyes from the light. A few moments pass, until I feel the light begin to fade. Removing my hand from my eyes, I blink intensely as I try to regain my sight and adjust to my surroundings. I am no longer in the temple of Delphi. In front of me, a layout of twelve thrones; the throne in the middle was adorned in gold, with blue canopy over the top, mirroring the sky. On the right arm of the throne was an eagle made up of gold with bright ruby eyes. Another throne directly next to it was made of ivory, with a white cow skin draped over the top. Down either side of the thrones are a further ten thrones, five on each side.

Behind me lies an enormous courtyard, with golden pavements that lead into every direction. On either side, smooth, verdant lawns stretched away. One segment held a large apple tree, its branches sagging beneath a heavy load of fruit.

Where am I?

As if hearing my thoughts, a tall glowing figure appears in front of me, sitting on the biggest throne in the middle of the room.

'Welcome to Mount Olympus,' welcomes the man in a loud, deafening voice.

Others start appearing, occupying the other thrones in the room, as if what he announced was a beckoning call.

Zeus? The king of all the gods.

Realising where I was, I quickly kneel before the gods of Mount Olympus.

'Rise, my daughter,' commands Zeus.

I do as I am told, shaking to the very centre of my bones, as I lift my face towards the twelve Olympian gods. The awe of their presence was captivating, entrancing. The idea of being in the very presence of these superior beings was enough to shake anyone to their core. I don't know how I should be feeling—confused, anxious, scared? In ancient times, no mortal could ever set foot on Olympus, but as times have developed, the gods have given an exception to only demigods and heroes.

'Do not be afraid . . . We are aware that you visited the oracle of Delphi, and in doing so, you have woken up the prophecy that we have all been dreading to hear,' Zeus explains.

'With the fate of Olympus in the hands of four demigods,' responds the god to the left of Zeus, holding a trident, Poseidon.

The gods start chatting amongst themselves, as if forgetting that I am still standing in front of them.

'Well, we've found one of the demigods, just three more to go,' Poseidon continues.

'The children of Zeus, Poseidon, Hades, and Apollo,' says an extremely beautiful Greek goddess, which I believe to have been Aphrodite.

'This means we need to invite Hades to our little reunion,' points out one of the gods.

'Agreed.'

'Hermes, send a message to the underworld,' Zeus commands as a letter appears in Hermes's hand. Hermes obeys his command and disappears, reappearing a few seconds later with another man. The man is clothed in a black robe from head to toe, holding a bident, resembling a pitchfork, with two pointed ends; his face not visible but hidden in the dark fog surrounding his body.

'Hades,' Zeus says, acknowledging his brother, as everyone brings their attention to the gloomy man who had immediately been summoned.

'We are putting the fate of Olympus in the hands of mortals?! This has to be the most horrendous thing I have heard in this century,' Hades says in a croaky voice as if he hadn't spoken in years.

'Father, you have very little faith in us.'

I freeze, not realising the presence of someone standing directly behind me. He walks forward, standing in line with me, before he turns to face me.

He has the kind of face that would stop you in your tracks, his raven black hair laying just above his shoulders, framing his carefully-structured face. He turns his attention back to the gods. His skin pale, like he had never seen the sun, and his eyes, they were chilling and dark.

He crosses his arms over his broad chest, tightening his black shirt on his body, revealing his muscled figure underneath.

'Alexandros Papatonis, you can't be serious?'

'You have never left the underworld. How can I put my trust in someone who knows little of the world above?' Hades replies harshly.

'What I cannot comprehend is that these mortals are too young, with very little experience of the real world,' explains Hermes.

'How old are you, my dear?' asks Aphrodite.

'Twenty,' replies Alexandros.

'My point exactly,' Hermes pushes his argument.

'A prophecy has been spoken, and we must take heed the words of the oracle. Age makes no difference when it comes to prophecies,' Poseidon demands.

As if the universe agreed with Poseidon, bright light appears before us all, slowly forming into two more figures.

CHAPTER 4

⌒◦⌒

Two Becomes Four

A man and a woman appear in front of us.

'Anastasia Papathanasiou.' Poseidon smiles as he notices the girl.

'Theodore Drakos.' Apollo grunts, narrowing his eyes at the sight of the boy.

The daughter of Poseidon and son of Apollo kneel before the gods.

The daughter of Poseidon had a kind of understated beauty; perhaps it was because she was aware of her prettiness. Her sun-kissed skin was completely flawless, her long wavy chestnut hair braided neatly over her left shoulder, her eyes framed with long lashes wearing a light-blue summer dress that lies just above her knees, leaving her toned figure visible.

The son of Apollo, tall, his features were alluring; his face well defined with a sharp jaw and angular cheekbones; his ocean blue eyes cold as ice; his golden blonde hair, short and styled, went well with his tanned skin; wearing a black leather jacket with cargo pants.

As they stand up, the son of Apollo turns and notices Alexandros and I, furrowing his eyebrows at him, a disapproving look evident on his face.

'What?' protests Alexandros.

Theodore shifts his attention to the gods and ignores his question.

'I prove my point—these mortals don't look like they have ever picked up a weapon in their lives,' complains Hades.

We all stay silent, not wishing to speak back to the god of the underworld.

'What more can we do? The oracle has given us a prophecy, and we must send these four demigods on the quest,' Zeus responds, looking at each of us judgingly.

Once again, the gods start arguing amongst themselves.

'ENOUGH!' Zeus roars as he stands up, looking at each of the gods in disappointment.

As he raises a hand, Zeus commands, 'Να φύγει.' *Be gone.*

White fog covers us. As it fades, we appear back at the temple of Delphi.

CHAPTER 5

Z for Zorander

'Well, that's just . . . great' murmurs Theodore as he throws his hands into the air in frustration.

'Hi, my name is Anastasia, but please call me Tia.' She stretches her hand out towards me. I return her gesture. 'Nice to meet you. Iris Dimitriadis,' I say as I introduce myself to the group.

'How exactly are we supposed to protect Olympus, and by whom?' questions Theodore.

He was right. We were not given any kind of instructions or the slightest hint to help assist us on this quest, just a pat on the back with a farewell.

'Four demigods, the offspring of each of the gods Zeus, Poseidon, Hades, and Apollo, none older than the age of twenty-five, will either bring chaos or raise Mount Olympus from the hold of evil,' I mumble to myself, not realising that I had very well said it loud enough that the others hear.

'Unanswered question is still in the air . . . save Olympus from what?' questions Alexandros.

'Doom, boy! Have you been living under the earth all this time? Zorander has been kidnapping young demigods and training them for years now,' Theodore says sarcastically. Alexandros rolls his eyes in response, not giving into him.

'Enough of that . . . and come again, who's Zorander?' I ask.

Tia answers me. 'Zorander is known as the most wicked demigod this century. He's always had it out for the gods, wanting to overthrow them as they did not make him immortal over a good deed he did a couple of years ago . . . also known to be incredibly dangerous.' She continues, 'Not only that, but I hear the demigods he kidnaps are trained as hunters to find more demigods to expand his army. The oracle must sense a war coming, which is why we received our prophecy.'

'How does he get away with it?'

Theodore answers me. 'He's manipulative. He will try his utter best to convince you that the gods aren't who they say they are. Plus, try to remember that half of these demigods were taken as children.'

First thirty minutes of being together and Theodore has already become a headache.

'Okay, so from the sound of things, all we need to do is defeat Zorander and stop his uprising against the gods?' says Alexandros. 'Easy.' He smirks.

'Hate to state the obvious, but it's almost three in the morning. Where are we supposed to go?' I ask.

They all turn and face me. 'The Olympic Sanctuary.'

The Olympic Sanctuary, a school for the offspring of the Olympian gods. Where demigods are trained daily for the threats of the outside world, learn about their history and their godly parents. A place where they are shielded from the eyes of mortals.

CHAPTER 6

The Sanctuary

Reaching the main road, Tia manages to wave down a taxi to take us to the sanctuary.

No, not a *regular* taxi. This one is operated by the Olympic service, specifically designed to transport demigods to wherever they desire to go.

Theo and Tia inform me on the Olympic Sanctuary during our drive. It's a safe haven for people like us, demigods. It keeps us protected from the outside world and its threats, i.e., monsters and people with bad intentions.

The sanctuary is located near Delphi, in Greece, but it cannot be found by a human. You must be a demigod to be accepted through the magical barrier protecting the sanctuary from the eyes of mortals.

So basically, I should have gone to school there, but that is beside the point. My aunt Maria had no idea the place existed.

I grew up in the small town of Monemvasia with my aunt Maria and cousin Darius. She has looked after me for as long as I can remember. I grew up homeschooled during my younger years, which I enjoyed immensely. But I did envy the kids who could go to school and make new friends, and after years of constantly harassing my aunt, I was eventually allowed to attend a public school for the last three years of my schooling. But my aunt Maria had a reasonable reason to which I was not allowed to attend school. She was afraid of the disappearance of children/teens in our hometown, which now we know is linked to Zorander.

I graduated high school one year ago. Since then, I have been working with my cousin Darius in their family-owned restaurant. Darius is not a demigod, but he knows the secrets of the Ancient Greek world.

'We're here!' exclaims Tia.

Looking out the taxi window reveals a wide gravel road leading towards a huge iron gate, but this gate looked more than an average iron gate, as grey mist swirled around it *(a barrier between the mystical and the norm)*.

What was beyond the gate, I could not tell, as the path beyond stretched onward, it seemed to not end. In the distance, the sound of howling wolves fill the early morning air.

As the taxi driver drove towards the iron gate, seconds within reaching it, the gate opens inwards, letting us pass through.

Driving up the gravel road, the sun began to rise, bringing life into the trees that were placed on either side of the road.

After driving for a few minutes, ahead of us lay a huge stone/marble mansion. The front of the mansion, in the inner courtyard, lay a huge water fountain; the water fell gently towards the crystal pool beneath it, causing ripples to form and wave out until they were no more. We all got out of the taxi, gaping at the mansion that was in front of us. It towered over us, making us feel like ants, attempting to intimidate us. The roof was peaked, slanting down at an angle. The windows had white curtains, the light from inside peeking through.

Looking around, I see the neatly-trimmed healthy green hedges that surround the mansion.

The door to the mansion swings open before us. Standing in the doorway was a middle-aged man in a pearl-white colored suit, which is quite unusual at this time. The hour did not faze him, as he looked more alive than ever, as he smiles at us with open arms.

'Welcome. We've been waiting for you,' says the man in the white suit as he gestured for all of us to follow him inside.

As I step inside the magnificent mansion, glancing around the place, the white marble floor glowed, as if it had just been recently cleaned. In front of me, a huge staircase that led into a huge room above.

Above me, a huge crystal chandelier dangled from the ceiling.

'Right this way,' led the man in the pearl-white suit.

He ascended the stairs; we followed close behind him. Upstairs led into a huge open room. The only furniture in the room was a round black marble table with dark chairs around it.

The man in the white suit sat opposite us all, on the other side of the table. 'How rude of me. My name is Mr. Hargreaves. Welcome to the Olympic Sanctuary,' he says, only looking at me. I respond with a simple smile. 'So, anything new?' he asks, looking towards Alexandros, Tia, and Theodore.

'Oh, nothing much. Just took an unexpected visit to Mount Olympus, received a prophecy, and now we're here,' mumbles Alexandros.

'What?' asks Mr. Hargreaves in disbelief.

'We were given a prophecy,' repeats Theodore.

'And what was it?'

They all turn and look at me. Rolling my eyes, I answer, 'Really, I'm the only one who remembers?'

Receiving no reply, I carry on.

When rain falls in cloudless skies, Olympus will be known once more. I warn you, the souls of the dead and the living will see no peace until Olympus is saved or razed to the ground. Four demigods, the offspring of each of the gods Zeus, Poseidon, Hades, and Apollo, none older than the age of twenty-five, will either bring chaos or raise Mount Olympus from the hold of evil.'

Mr. Hargreaves stares at me blankly. Without even blinking.

'Sir?' I ask, trying to get him to respond.

'Ah . . . um . . . well, I see,' he manages to choke out. 'But you guys are an odd bunch to receive a quest.'

'Trust us, we know,' huffs Tia.

'Well, I guess there is no time to waste. You must start preparing!' he responds before jumping up from his seat and walks towards a corridor.

We all get up in unison and follow him. The corridor leads into another room with an open balcony. He walks towards the balcony.

As I reach the balcony, I look around, taking in all my surroundings. In front of us lay four buildings, in a horseshoe formation facing the mansion. The buildings look like the mansion, just a lot smaller, made from brick, with green vines that clung to the sides of the houses.

Far off into the distance, there were a couple more buildings; one looked like a stable and the other an arena. They even have a tennis court, the fake grass bright as the sun shone over it.

Behind the stables lay the beach, the sun glistening on the sand off into the horizon, the water sparkled, dolphins flip into the air then retreat into the ocean.

'Come on, I'll show you to your rooms,' said Mr. Hargreaves.

CHAPTER 7

Work for It

M r. Hargreaves directs us all to our rooms before leading us over to the cafeteria for breakfast.

The cafeteria looks like an average university cafeteria, with long wooden tables and a few middle-aged women serving the food from behind the counter.

The Olympic Sanctuary was finally awake; children, teens, and young adults fill the cafeteria with chatter. No one paid attention to us. They must have a regular number of newcomers that it does not faze them anymore.

I stand in the queue with my tray, followed by the others. Everywhere I looked, there were stacks of food; one section, a continental breakfast, the other toast and toppings. I did not know where to start. I notice a few of the younger demigods backing away, keeping a safe distance from Alexandros, their faces plastered with fear.

After choosing my breakfast from a vast variety of food, I take a seat at an empty table.

My stomach grumbles. I did not realise how hungry I was. Spreading the avocado on top of my sourdough bread and scrambled eggs, I begin to eat my breakfast.

★☆★

After we had finished eating, Theodore led us to the sanctuary's library.

Inside the library was silent; all you could hear were the faint chirps of birds outside and children laughing as they played.

Inside had row after row of neatly lined books with their spines facing outward.

'Look for the book of missing demigods. It should be called *Forgotten Souls,*' suggests Theodore.

After some time of walking along the long aisles, for the letter F, I came across the book—"*Forgotten Souls.*

'Here, I found it.'

Theodore takes the book from my hands, flipping the book open, carefully looking through each of the pages.

'Ah ha!' he exclaims with a huge smile. 'Here!'

He points at one of the headings; it read, 'Missing Orphans.'

'What is it?' I question the list in front of me.

'This is the list of children that are known to be taken by Zorander.'

My eyes widen as I realise how many names were written under the heading. 'There are so many,' I gasp.

'Exactly, so this uprising . . . it's going to be a horrific one.'

To my amazement, I see another name magically start to scribble on the end of the list.

'What? No . . . He's gotten another one,' I gasp.

'And there's only four of us,' Tia mumbles as she appears with Alexandros from one of the aisles. Walking towards us, she presents a book. 'We found this book too. It explains that it's really rare for a demigod to be a child of the top three gods, let alone three of them participating on a quest.'

She pauses. 'Sorry, Theo—I mean, Theodore,' she quickly adds.

He smiles at her. 'You can call me Theo.' She blushes at his response.

Alexandros rolls his eyes at them and continues, 'So the kids on this list, shouldn't be children from Zeus, Poseidon, or Hades. This does give us a huge advantage.'

Wait a second.

I guess you are asking yourself, why is it unlikely for the top three gods to have more than one child per century? Well, the answer is they're too dangerous.

"The Big Three are the three most powerful gods in all of Olympus—Zeus, Hades, and Poseidon. Their demigod children are far more powerful than any other demigod. This is the exact reason the top three gods only have one child per human lifetime. We can be a danger to the human race, our strength is legendary, and frightening towards anyone that isn't on our side." Tia informs me, as she tells me the values of the children of the top three gods.

There are plenty of demigods/half-bloods, but they are offspring of deities and spirits. The ten Olympian gods are Hera, Apollo, Athena, Artemis, Aphrodite, Ares, Demeter, Hephaestus, Hermes, and Hestia. Demigod children from the ten Olympians receive their supernatural powers within their early teen years.

A child from the top three Olympians—Zeus, Poseidon, and Hades— do not receive theirs until they reach the age of eighteen and later. Okay, back to the story.

'It's also believed that Zorander has his army located within the Bermuda Triangle,' Alexandros says, showing an A4 piece of paper, which reads 'Z-Biography.'

'Okay, so we have our destination. We just need our transportation.'

CHAPTER 8

Bow or Sword

'Come on, this way to the weapon shed,' Mr. Hargreaves interrupts us as he walks into the library.

'Please tell me you have bows,' Theo asks eagerly.

'Yes, and much more,' he replies as he leads us out of the library towards an old rustic shed.

The shed was right next to the training arena, where we could see teenagers training against one another using swords, knives, and anything that is classified as a weapon. To the right lay the archery field, where heaps of demigods where training with their bows, aiming at electronically-moving targets.

'Here we are,' Mr. Hargreaves says as he opens the hatch on the shed door, letting us inside. 'I will leave you in the hands of Jake,' he says as he motions towards a guy on the other side of the shed, sharpening a heat-treated sword.

The inside of the weapon shed was brightly lit by a furnace in the far-left corner of the room, with all types of various weapons hanging on the metallic walls of the shed.

'Hi, Jake,' says Theo as he extends his hand towards the boy so that he would notice us.

Jake looks up, ruffing up his dirty blonde hair, before shaking Theo's extended hand. The boy's ocean blue eyes shone with kindness as he smiled at us.

'Hey, you must be here for your weapons,' he replies.

'Yes, we are,' I say with a nod. Our eyes connect for a few seconds before he quickly turns away, clearing his throat.

'All right, let me work my magic.'

Jake looks us all up and down, with his hands on his hips as he studies us. Rubbing his chin with his hand, 'Son of Apollo, you're an archer,' he says, walking around Theo.

'No . . . way,' Theo responds sarcastically.

Jake makes his way over to me, studying me, which makes me shift uncomfortably on the spot. 'Daughter of Zeus, swordsman.'

'Swordsman?' I ask.

He looks at me with a frown, as if I had asked the dumbest question. 'Are you questioning me?' he asks, crossing his hands over his chest.

'Um . . . no. But how can you possibly know?'

'I'm the son of Hephaestus,' and that was all he needed to say. The god Hephaestus is the god of fire, metalworking, blacksmiths, forging, and masonry. He passes on these traits to his children, demigods.

He moves on to Alexandros. 'Impossible . . . I'm receiving nothing from you,' he says in disbelief.

'Son of Hades. I don't need a specialised weapon.'

Jake nods understandingly before he points towards Tia and says, 'Daughter of Poseidon, you will be receiving a sword also.'

Tia does not question the boy but nods in agreement.

'Excellent,' Jake responds. He turns around looking at all the weapons hanging on the wall before grabbing a metallic-looking bow and a quiver with only one arrow, handing it to Theo.

'What? Only one arrow?' scolds Theo.

'Take the arrow out and place it on the bow string and see what happens?' answers Jake.

As Theo takes the arrow from the quiver, another instantly replaces it.

'I can work with this,' Theo says obviously impressed.

'This bow, I specially designed for a child of Apollo. The arrows can shoot powerful rays of sunlight . . . so be careful.'

Jake grabs a longsword from the wall. 'This sword is made from Damascus steel. It has a doubled-edged blade. I also managed to tinker with it so it's light and easy to swing,' he says, handing me the sword.

I thank him as I reach out, retrieving it from his hand. It was light, easy to carry. I turn it around in my hand, marveling the craftsman's skill. The silver blade was smooth and glinted beneath the light.

'That sword can also withstand the power of lightning,' he adds before turning his attention towards Tia.

'And lucky last, I have just the sword for you . . . I do not like to admit this, but I found it in one of the ocean caves along the beach. So, it must be fit for a daughter of Poseidon.'

Jake goes to the bench top where he was previously standing at and picks up an arming sword that he was previously working on; this sword was shorter than the one I received. 'I have managed to polish and grind away the stones that was on the blade, so it's as good as new.'

Tia thanks him as she takes the sword from his hand.

Before walking off to have lunch, Jake stops me.

'Daughter of Zeus, I will be training you at noon, so meet me at the fighting arena.'

CHAPTER 9

Practice Makes Perfect

The others were born natural fighters. For Tia and Theo, this was not their first quest. They acquired their first prophecies at the age of sixteen. Theo participated on retrieving the 'Golden Fleece' that was placed by Aeetes in a secret garden guarded by a dragon that never rests, which is now kept here at the Olympic Sanctuary, as Tia and two other demigods went on a quest to save a fellow centaur from the hands of Cyclopes.

After lunch, I went back towards the fighting arena, where I find Jake leaning against the fence, waiting for me.

It is a warm summer's day here in αγιοι παντες *(Agioi Pantes, Delphi)* as the sun shines brightly from the heavens, no cloud in sight.

'Hey,' I say, reaching him.

'Ready?' he asks, straightening his posture, picking up my longsword and another similar one that was leaning against the fence beside him.

I nod in agreement as I retrieve my sword from him.

'All right, it's going to just be you and me, to save you from embarrassment.'

'Wow, okay. You have little faith in me,' I respond with a chuckle.

As he opens the gate towards the fighting arena, he turns back and gives me a smile.

I follow Jake inside. To my left, I see Theo with his new bow at the archery field, aiming at one of the moving targets. He releases the arrow as it zips through the air, hitting the bull's eye.

'He's a natural,' Jake says as he catches me watching Theo.

'His father is Apollo after all,' I respond.

Once I was standing in the centre of the arena, Jake turns standing in a fighting stance, sword pointing towards me.

'I want you to copy my stance.'

I reflect his on-guard position as I extend my hand, readjusting my grip on my one-handed longsword.

'Excellent. Now when I thrust my sword towards you, block it with yours,' he explains.

'Okay, sounds straightforward,' I answer.

We circle each other before Jake thrusts his sword towards my stomach, but I manage to block his attack.

I slide to the left, keeping a safe distance between Jake and I before I thrust my sword towards him. Our blades clash as Jake blocks my sword, spinning it around and throwing it into the air.

'Better, but not good enough,' he says as he retrieves my sword from the ground, returning it to me.

'Now let's try that again,' he says. Our blades clash, and my sword goes spinning through the air again . . . and again . . . and again . . . and again.

We continued until dusk as I was not going to quit without a fight.

Our blades clashed again, but this time it was Jake's sword that went flying through the air, to my great pleasure.

'What the heck! No one has mastered the skills of sword fighting so quickly,' Jake exclaims. 'But you can't expect much less from a daughter of Zeus,' he adds with a chuckle.

CHAPTER 10

The Minotaur

The night consisted of us trying to obtain information about the Bermuda Triangle. But the sanctuary's library had limited information about Ancient Greek ships strong enough to withstand the waves within the outer realms of the triangle.

No one dared to go that far. Anyone that did try never returned.

But we did manage to stumble across the most well-known ship in Ancient Greece, the *Argo*.

'It reads here that the *Argo*'s last known resting place is somewhere in the North Atlantic Ocean near the East Coast of the United States of America,' states Tia. Looking up from the book in her hands, she continues, "To be more precise, I've come across ancient stories that the ship was sunk at the bottom of the ocean east of Charleston, South Carolina.'

'But I thought that ship was destroyed after Jason and the Argonauts used it,' Theo responds.

'No not exactly . . . you see, the goddess of wisdom, Athena, helped Argus with the construction of the *Argo*, so it's the fastest and strongest ship known in Greece. The ship was designed to outmaneuver other vessels in the ocean. It can't possibly be destroyed,' mentions Alexandros.

'Okay, so if the ship is still out there, how are we supposed to reach it?' I ask.

'We can't travel by plane or boat, as Zorander has eyes and ears everywhere. He would pick up on what we are doing if we take the obvious route. The only way we can reach South Carolina without Zorander knowing is by . . . ' Tia looks around nervously before continuing, 'We'd have to travel through the Labyrinth.'

'No way in hell will I be going in there!' Alexandros snaps.

'I hate to admit this, but I agree with Alexandros. The Labyrinth is too dangerous! We'd be writing our own death certificate if we take that route,' Theo exclaims.

'Someone fill me in. What's a labyrinth?' I ask curiously.

'Wait, you cannot be serious?' Tia says confused.

'Cut her some slack. She hasn't been brought up by Hades in the underworld or trained here at camp. But you do need to learn to open up a book about your history,' insists Theo.

'So, can we go back to explaining?'

'Wait, let me find a book. Trust me, it's easier to understand with pictures,' says Alexandros as he walks off into one of the aisles but returns quickly with a thin book in his hand. 'Here, read this. It explains the origins of the Labyrinth.'

I take the book from his hand, flipping it open to the first page.

I am not going to go into too much detail about the story of the Labyrinth in Crete. But let us say the labyrinth is designed to look like a maze. It was built by Daedalus for King Minos of Knossos in Crete to contain a half-man, half-bull creature, the Minotaur.

The legend goes that the Minotaur would only feed on human flesh, but because King Minos would not offer his own people as sacrifices, he taxed the city of Athens, asking that they send seven young men and seven young women to Crete every year, so that they would be sent into the Labyrinth to be eaten by the Minotaur.

Let us just say that King Minos was smart; he gave them hope by mentioning that if any of them could defeat the Minotaur, they would be rewarded with great riches.

I am not going to mention how the Minotaur was created, but if you are still itching about it later, just take out your smartphone and search up '*the Minotaur and the Labyrinth of Crete*.' Trust me, you would question the actions of the Greek gods, not going to name any names but I would never want to cross paths with Poseidon.

'Well, that explains why you don't want to travel through the Labyrinth.'

Alexandros nods in agreement. 'And that's not the worst part—the Labyrinth continually changes, so the path to get out is never the same.'

CHAPTER 11

Ask Away

The silence in the library was deafening, no one wished to speak, as the thought of doing so, they would crumble on the impact of someone's opinion.

Even though Theo and Alexandros mentioned why they wish not to travel through the Labyrinth, Tia seemed unfazed by it all.

The idea of travelling through an endless maze, which constantly changes underneath the earth's surface, is frightening.

'There is a way we can travel through the Labyrinth,' Tia manages to slice through the silence.

'How do you suppose we do that?' Alexandros snorts.

'Easy, we have you.'

We all turn our attention to Alexandros. In defeat, he throws his hands up in the air.

'He can help us navigate through the maze. You can summon one of the hellhounds from the underworld. The hound can lead us through the Labyrinth.' When no one interrupts her, she continues on. 'This Labyrinth is not an ordinary Labyrinth, as it's mystical. It has many entries and exits that stretch throughout the world. We just need to find the one closest to our location and then find an exit as close as we can to South Carolina without running into the Minotaur.'

'How would the one Minotaur find us in such a huge Labyrinth?'
I ask.

'As a spider knows when its prey is caught in its web, so does the
Minotaur know as soon as one enters its lair,' answers Theo.

'I don't like this, but I suppose it's the only plan we have,' responds
Alexandros as he slumps down in one of the chairs, crossing his arms
over his chest. 'Where's the closest entrance?'

We scan the ancient text in the book. After some time, Tia
shouts, 'Mount Giona in Kallii. That's only 72 kilometres away if we
travel by the Olympic taxi.'

And in case you were wondering, the Olympic taxi cannot take us to
America as it cannot leave Greece.

'From the looks of things, I guess there is no other way,' I admit
as I accept the circumstances.

'Looks like we're taking the death route,' Theo finally gives in.

Grabbing the map of the Labyrinth off the table in front of me, I
look for the closest exits to South Carolina.

'So this map shows that the closest exit to South Carolina is in
New York,' I say, pointing to the location on the map.

'Okay, if we don't die before we reach New York, we will need
to make our way to the location of the *Argo*. There, we will need to
find a way to resurface the ship from the bottom of the ocean. This
is where Tia will come in handy,' Theo says, winking at the shy girl
beside him. 'But . . . what stops us in our tracks is that we lack a crew
or a way to repair and strengthen the *Argo* to withstand the Bermuda
Triangle,' he explains.

'You can cross out "crew" from that list. I've got that part covered,'
responds Alexandros. I raise an eyebrow at the son of Hades, which
he simple responds with a smirk.

'I'm confused. What abilities do you all possess?' I ask, eager to
find out their strengths.

'I'm glad you asked,' Theo begins. 'As the son of Apollo, god of
the sun, poetry, healing, and archery, I possess his abilities also. I
can heal or curse someone with incredible illness, my archery skills

cannot be compared to another, and I can also produce an extremely high-pitched whistle,' he boasts proudly.

'That's amazing,' I respond with a smile. 'What about you, Tia?'

'As the daughter of Poseidon, the god of the sea, I can manipulate and control water, generate earthquakes and hurricanes,' she says shyly, unlike Theo, not wishing to boast about her strengths.

'Wow' was all I could manage to say.

I turn to Alexandros, silently asking for him to continue on.

'Well . . . my father, being the god of the underworld, has passed on the traits of communication and control of the dead.' He stops and waits for me to process what he just said before continuing, 'I can shadow travel, something I'd rather not do, if I can avoid. It drains a lot of my strength. In times of need, I can also use *dark magic*. Yep, that sums me up!' The way he spoke was like he was ashamed of having this much strength, as if being a child of Hades automatically made you *evil*.

The way the children at the sanctuary avoided him as he walks past, it must be instinct for him to speak as if he frightened his audience. Being a demigod that others feared, being a son of a god, most people hate, and having all that consuming you, just because your father is the god of the underworld, he doesn't deserve this.

I respond with a polite smile, 'Does anyone know what a child of Zeus possesses?' I ask, 'What am I capable of?'

They turn to one another before shaking their heads 'no.'

'We've never encountered a daughter of Zeus here at the sanctuary before,' Theo responds. 'I guess we have to wait and see.'

'I guess we will . . .,' I respond half-heartedly.

I look between Tia and Alexandros, 'Does that mean we are cousins?'

'No.' Tia quickly responds, 'no, that does not mean we are related . . .'

'But—'

Alexandros interrupts me, 'Yes our fathers are biologically brothers, but their blood relation doesn't pass on to us. If they did, we would all be related in some sort of way.'

'I see . . . ' I answer.

'So back to the *Argo*, I'm guessing we will need a child of Hephaestus, one that has the ability to repair and strengthen the *Argo*?' Tia asks. 'Looks like we need to convince Jake to tag along,' she suggests.

'We can't pursue this plan without him. He now plays a significant role in our quest . . . " Alexandros groans, holding up his forehead with the palm of his hands.

'I can't stand that guy,' hisses Theo. 'He acts like a know-it-all, and it's pathetic.'

Tia chuckles. 'To me, it sounds like you're . . . jealous.'

'Shut up!' Theo snaps.

'I'll do it,' I say, breaking the tension between the two. 'I'll ask Jake.'

CHAPTER 12

The Unforgivable

E ven though it was late, the others still insisted I go speak to Jake
ASAP. As Theo stated, 'This is more important than beauty sleep.'

The night air was cool against my bare arms. I should have grabbed my jacket. Luckily for me, the lit torches set up around the camp chase the shadows away that lurk around every corner.

I make my way over to the weapons shed, guessing he would still be in there.

I freeze on the spot, hesitant to knock on the door of the shed. I let out the breath of air I did not realise I was holding in and knock.

If I were in his shoes, I would not volunteer to help on a quest nor jump at the idea of being asked to do so. The whole idea of a prophecy was unfortunate for a demigod. So, if you were not given one, you were considered 'lucky.' No one in their right mind would willingly volunteer to help assist on a quest.

The door to the shed swings open, releasing me from my thoughts as I lock eyes with Jake.

'Umm . . . Hi,' I manage to let out.

'What's up?' he asks, stepping aside, letting me in.

'I need to ask you something important.'

'Go on.'

'The team and I need your help. We need you to come along with us on our quest. We are leaving tomorrow at the crack of dawn.'

Jake stares at me in disbelief. 'No.' He takes a few steps away from me, as if distance could save him from me.

'You haven't given me the chance to explain,' I urge.

'And? I'm not going to change my answer.'

'Please, just listen to what I have to say before you make a decision,' I plea.

He stares at me intently before giving in. 'Fine.'

'We've figured that the only way we can reach the Bermuda Triangle is by taking the *Argo*.' I pause. After receiving no response from Jake, I continue, 'And we need you to . . . to help improve the *Argo* before we take it out to sea.'

He raises his eyebrow but continues to listen.

'The *Argo* is somewhere near the East Coast of South Carolina, and the only way to reach it unnoticed is to travel through the Labyrinth . . . If you don't help us, the chances of us all making it alive are reduced.'

His eyes widen in shock. 'No! How could you even ask me that?' he snaps.

'But—'

'I said no!'

There was no chance that I could change his mind; he was set against it. We could not possibly expect him to drop everything and come.

Fear finally creeps its way into my mind as I question the ability of us completing this quest. We really need the luck of the gods on our side if we are ever going to make it out alive. Pushing the fearful thoughts away, I return to reality.

Turning to leave, I face him once more. 'Everything aside, I really hope you change your mind.'

And with that, I left.

CHAPTER 13

The Start

T he world is silent, as if it had ended during the night.

I am woken up by the sunlight that shines beneath my bedroom door, giving the window shutters a form of halo rays. I close my eyes, as I feel my dreams trying to pull me back to sleep, until the thought of today penetrated it.

I slowly sit myself up on the bed, giving myself a moment to shed the sleep from my mind, stretching my arms above my head, letting out a yawn, as I dangle my legs above the wooden floorboards.

Today was the beginning of it all— the start of our prophecy.

I slowly make my way over to the combined washroom, where I am greeted by Tia as she brushes her hair. She wore black sports leggings with a dark-blue cropped-top sweater, looking like one of those influencers you see online.

'Morning!' she says way too cheerfully.

'Morning . . .,' I mumble.

I stand in front of one of the washroom mirrors. Turning on the tap, I wash the sleep from my face.

I position myself in front of the mirror. As a young girl, I never bothered with makeup. I did not need it. But right now, my lips could use a bit of gloss. I lick my bottom lip, giving it a bit of shine. I run my fingers, detangling my long chocolate brown hair. My olive-colored skin, visible as I still had my pajama shorts on.

Returning to my room, I slip on some white sneakers and change into a white T-shirt, tucking it into my ripped light-blue jeans.

I take a deep breath, trying to settle the nerves in my stomach. Grabbing my black leather jacket, I walk out of the bedroom. Looking around, I see the morning sun begin to rise, the fresh morning air smelling like the ocean.

'Ready?' Alexandros says as he walks out of one of the rooms, wearing a full-black outfit: pants, top, and leather jacket.

'As ready as I'll ever be.'

Theo and Tia emerge from their rooms also.

'Hi, guys, wonderful morning!' exclaims Theo.

No one responds.

'Let's grab some things before we go,' he continues.

We grab some breakfast before packing some bags with essentials, i.e., food, money, and our weapons.

We then make our way towards the front gates of the sanctuary.

★☆★

'Wait!'

We all stop in our tracks and turn towards the direction of the voice, seeing that it belongs to Jake.

Hope.

My heart relaxes in my chest. I can breathe again.

'Jake?' I ask as he runs towards us, wearing white denim shorts and a blue muscle tee, looking the part of a cliché surfer boy.

'Change of heart?' Theo snorts.

Jake does not reply; he stops right in front of us, leaning on his knees as he catches his breath. 'You can't save someone from their destiny or from what they were created to complete. All you can do is help make it easier for them . . . If you still need me, I'd like to tag along.'

A smile creeps its way onto my face. 'Yes!' I blurt out.

'Really?!'

'Yeah, I guess we could use your help.' Alexandros laughs.

A huge burden was lifted within the group and replaced by hope—we had a fighting chance.

CHAPTER 14

❧

Olympic Taxi

W e manage to flag down an Olympic taxi to take us towards Mount Giona.

The taxi stops right in front of a gravel path that leads towards the foot of the mountain. We pay the taxi driver with a few drachmas before exiting the car.

'What does the entrance to the Labyrinth look like?' I ask, retrieving my sword's scabbard from the boot of the taxi and attaching it to my belt.

Tia and Theo mimic my actions as they do the same with their weapons, grabbing their quiver and scabbard.

'You'll know when you see it,' Alexandros responds, grabbing a backpack, using one of the straps to hold it over his right shoulder.

'That works,' huffs Theo as he heads down the gravel road.

We follow the path for a few miles before we are stopped by a river that flows over the path. The river winds through the mountain, welcoming stray flora that comes its way. It had strength that was reflected in the trees as it flows onward with confidence.

'Do you see that?' cries Tia.

'See what?'

'The green mist that flows against the river.'

Facing my attention towards the river, I see what she means, green mist hovers over the river but leads the opposite direction of the water flow.

'This way!' Alexandros exclaims as he follows the direction of the mist.

The mist leads towards a large rock boulder before it ends, and just like that, gone.

It did not leave us time to question what was happening as the dark green mist forms into a hollow entrance through the rock.

'Bingo!' shouts Tia in excitement.

The dark entrance was not welcoming at all, cold air coming from inside it, chasing away the sunny day, making us shiver on the spot.

I look around at the others nervously, rubbing away the goosebumps on my arms.

'I'll lead,' Alexandros says as he carelessly walks towards the hollow entrance.

'Wait—'

He does not listen as the mist dissolves him and disappears.

'Oh sh*t,' gasps Jake.

'Come on, we can't leave him in there all by himself,' Tia states the obvious before following Alexandros's lead and entering the mist.

Theo rushes into the mist behind her, believing the faster he got in there, the quicker it was all over with.

Jake turns to face me; his bright blue eyes filled with horror. 'Ladies first,' he tries to lighten the mood.

I smile at him, ensuring that there was nothing to worry about.

'See you on the other side,' I tease before walking into the chillingly cold entrance.

CHAPTER 15

Hellhound

The inside of the labyrinth was dark, with only a few lit torches hanging against the walls. The walls were a dark grey stone covered with moss and towered above at a good twenty feet, each wall identical to the next, without an identifying mark of any kind.

Behind me, Jake stumbles out of the mist.

'Glad you could join us,' Theo mentions, as Jake regains his composure.

'I don't want to do that again . . .'

Alexandros clears his throat to grab everyone's attention before stating, 'I need to call our tour guide.'

'What?' asks Jake.

'You didn't think we'd come into the labyrinth without a plan, did you?' Theo snickers.

Both Theo and Alexandros were coming out of their shells and becoming know-it-alls towards Jake. He ignores the boy's remarks.

'Jokes aside, I need everyone to be silent as I summon him . . . and when you see him, don't make any loud noises or sudden movements.'

Alexandros closes his eyes as he begins an Ancient Greek chant to summon his hellhound from the underworld.

His voice is dark and chilling. Ἀδης. άκου καθώς καλέσω το σκυλί από την κόλαση. Αφήστε τον να βγει από το σκοτάδι.' *Hades, listen as I summon the dog from hell. Let him emerge from the darkness.*

A shadowy darkness covers the area in front of Alexandros as it slowly forms into a dark creature. The hellhound's features were becoming visible as the shadow fades away. It has mangled black fur, dark glowing red eyes, looking surreal with its phantom, and ghostly features. The beast had three dog heads and a serpent tale.

I cover my mouth with my hands as I muffle the yelp that tries to escape.

Even though the hound was loyal to Alexandros, every time it growled, it sent shivers down my spine.

A hellhound is the offspring of Cerberus, the hound known by the Ancient Greeks as it guarded the underworld. Hellhounds are known to devour anyone that tries to leave or enter the underworld.

The hound jumps around, acting like a harmless puppy as soon as it notices Alexandros.

'Buddy! Long time no see,' Alexandros says as he lunges onto the hound, engulfing it with a hug.

'That's definitely something you don't see every day,' utters Theo.

'Shh, you're ruining the moment,' Tia says, giggling.

'What?' asks Alexandros as he brushes the fluff off his pants.

Tia and Theo respond with laughter.

'Whatever. You're just jealous you don't have a special bond with a hound,' mumbles Alexandros.

'All right, let's start walking before the walls begin to change,' insists Jake.

'Good plan . . . What does the houn—'

'Buddy. His name is Buddy!' Alexandros snaps, interrupting Theo. Buddy howls in agreement.

'Sorry . . . Buddy . . .,' apologises Theo.

'Buddy, I'm going to need you to go ahead and find us the exit portal for New York.'

The hound nods his three heads in agreement before disappearing into the shadows.

We all stand there patiently waiting for Alexandros's instructions. It seems like we've been waiting there for ages before Buddy reappears in front of us, growling.

'What is it, boy?

'Grrrrr.'

'Two days?'

'Grr . . . woof!'

'Okay, that can work. Did you see where?'

As Alexandros and Buddy are having their coded chat, the rest of us pull faces, trying to comprehend what is happening in front of us.

'Okay, good boy!' responds Alexandros as he pats the middle head of the hound. He turns around facing us before adding, 'Buddy mentioned that the trip to the New York portal exit is a two-day trip. So we have a long difficult trip ahead of us before we can set up camp for the night. But to make matters worse, Buddy can smell the Minotaur. It's on its way to intercept us.'

'You got all that from a "woof"?' asks Jake, looking back and forth between Alexandros and Buddy.

'A plus side from growing up in the underworld,' replies Alexandros.

'So where will we be setting up camp?' I ask.

Alexandros nods towards Buddy. 'We follow the tour guide.'

'But what about the Minotaur?' whimpers Jake.

No one replies as the thought terrified us.

Buddy looks towards Alexandros, waiting for his permission before leading us through the Labyrinth.

We all follow closely behind Alexandros and the hound in single file. Wherever we went, the walls stretch away from us as far as the eye could see.

Buddy leading us down, narrow, and wide paths, turning left, right, left, I lost track after some time.

'I'm just going to ask the question: How can Buddy navigate through . . . this place?' asks Jake.

'You and all your questions,' chimes in Theo.

Tia faces me and rolls her eyes at Theo's remark.

'Buddy can travel through the shadows of the Labyrinth at incredible speed. He can also feel when the Labyrinth changes and sense where the shadows point. He will always know where the exit is, even if the maze changes inside,' responds Alexandros.

After hours of travelling at a fast pace, as the fear of bumping into the Minotaur pumps us forward, we hear the Labyrinth changing. It's a loud, piercing, mechanical sound as the stone walls rumble as they move against one another.

Alexandros sighs a relief as we managed to pass through that section before the change and no Minotaur, but I fear that's only a matter of time before we come face-to-face with the monster himself.

CHAPTER 16

Double Standards

My legs begin to feel numb by the time we made it to a site that we can use to rest for the night. Buddy figured out that this part of the Labyrinth must be immune to the changes. I hope he is right.

The room was small. It looked identical to the rest of the Labyrinth, but it only had one entrance/exit from it.

'Home, sweet home.' Alexandros sighs, dropping his backpack and sitting on the ground.

Time was unknown in the Labyrinth as there was no day or night, just darkness, barely lit by a few torches.

'We will rest for a little bit, and then we can continue. We can't waste too much time. We will need to take turns keeping watch. Rather be safe than sorry,' suggests Tia.

'I'll take the first watch,' volunteers Jake.

We all set up sleeping bags, as comfortably as we could around the room, as Jake takes the first watch.

My eyes begin to feel heavier and heavier as I finally close my eyes, sending me off into a dreamless sleep.

★☆★

I wake up all alert as if it were an emergency, as if sleep had become a dangerous thing. I sit up, looking around to see that the others were still asleep, except for Alexandros as he sat near the entrance of the room, keeping watch.

Nearly time for my watch for the night, I rise from my sleeping bag and head towards Alexandros.

'Hi,' I whisper as I take a seat beside him.

'Couldn't sleep?'

'The ground isn't the comfiest thing. Any signs of the Minotaur?'

'Nope. Nothing at all.'

'I'll take the rest of your watch.'

Alexandros is hesitant before accepting my offer and rejoins the others.

I lean against the stone wall of the Labyrinth. Buddy came and sat down beside me before I let my thoughts entertain me.

Younger me would not expect for life to have taken such a turn. As far as I can remember, I would constantly ask my aunt where my father was, and her response constantly remained the same. 'He was not ready to be a father.' Up until my thirteenth birthday, the day I found out the whole truth, except my aunt left out one minor detail—who my father was.

That left me questioning my existence, as my father may not necessarily be a major Olympian god, but he could be a lesser one, such as a nymph. So the list of 'father figures' was endless.

The Greek gods had a very liberal attitude in life. Family reunions was not applicable to them as they had so many children. There was no point in getting to know them, especially if they had a short lifespan.

I never knew my mother. She passed away when I was only four years old, the result of a car crash. My aunt Maria has brought me up as her own ever since then, taking care of me and treating me as her very own daughter. I am truly grateful for her. With her boundaries and protection, she protected me from the harm of others. As she must have known deep down that I was not an average mortal, I feel she started to notice the changes of my abilities when I was sixteen years old. That was the age I noticed that something was different with me. I started showing signs of superhuman abilities, increased agility, strength, intelligence, and healing. I could heal at an incredible rate, which was totally unhuman. The fact that my aunt never met my father, the voice in the back of her head kept bugging her to send me to the oracle of Delphi to put her mind at ease.

Even though I am eighteen years old, I was forbidden to date. My aunt Maria believed it would be a distraction as she thought I would not achieve much if I were love-struck over some *useless* male. 'Love doesn't last,' she would constantly tell me. I think that it's partially related to the fact that her husband left her when she was pregnant with Darius for a much younger woman. But she did not have the same rules towards her own son Darius. He could go wherever he wanted, whenever he wanted, with whoever he wanted. *Double standards.*

He was considered one of those school players. He would jump from girl to girl and then when he got bored, throw them away as if they were candy wrappers. I, on the other hand, would keep my distance from that type of crowd. Everyone knew I was related to Darius, but they would not bat a single eye towards me. I blended right in, keeping my mind focused on my classes and obeying aunt Maria's words: *Focus on your grades, nothing else.* Well, I have to say I am grateful that she was strict with me. I accomplished much throughout school. But I never got to experience the average 'teen' life that you would see in movies.

Buddy growls from beside me, shaking me back to reality. I hear something off in the distance. I begin to panic.

I stumble to my feet, yelling to the others, 'Get up! We have to go. NOW! RIGHT NOW!'

CHAPTER 17

First Time for Everything

Everyone jumps up at once. We grab everything, and we run. Jake complains, 'What's the rush?'

'I think the Minotaur is here. Buddy can sense it closing in on us,' I reply. We all run faster than we have ever run before. We follow Buddy and Alexandros at a hectic pace forward through the Labyrinth.

'Stop!' yells Alexandros in a tone that made us all freeze on the spot. We see the expression on his face. It was like he had seen a ghost.

'What—"

'Shhhh,' Alexandros interrupts.

We all stand there in silence, frozen. Something was blocking our progress ahead.

'Can't you hear that?' Alexandros whispers.

Shaking my head as I did not want to hear it, as it could only be one thing.

How could it have gotten in front of us so quickly? I look around wide-eyed in horror. I bring my attention towards Alexandros. 'It can't be . . .'

The hairs on the back of Buddy's necks spring up, as his fangs emerge from his mouths, ready to protect us from the beast up ahead.

'Wait, what's going on?' screams Tia.

'The Minotaur, it's in front of us!' Alexandros snaps.

'We can't go any other way. We need to go directly towards the Minotaur and confront it,' I urge.

'What are we waiting for? It's just a Minotaur,' Theo says, taking the lead, heading directly towards the beast, simultaneously pulling the arrow from his quiver and readying his bow.

'Wait,' Tia says as she grabs his arm, stopping him from going any further.

He looks at her. Realising what she had done, she immediately releases his arm, facing away from him, embarrassed.

'Let's not rush into battle without being prepared,' I say, bringing the attention towards me.

'Let's get this over with,' Alexandros grumbles as he heads down the Labyrinth.

The closer we get towards the growls of the Minotaur, the more anxious I become.

The tight path of the Labyrinth opens into a huge room, with moss and vines growing on the walls and stone pillars. To the far-left corner was the doorway we needed to enter to be able to exit the Labyrinth and enter New York.

But one thing was blocking our path; in the middle of the room stood an enormous beast, *the Minotaur.*

The beast was huge and grotesque with matted hair and huge twisting horns protruding upward. The contorted figure visible, it stood on its knotted haunches. The beast stooped as its wrinkled face stares at me. It gave off an aura of death, its eyes dull, radiating pure evil; holding an enormous axe in its hand.

The Minotaur roars, shaking the walls of the Labyrinth.

I heard a little squeal from Jake. I think he sh*t his pants. I could smell a terrible smell. I don't know if it was Jake or the Minotaur. Actually, thinking about it, I think we all sh*t our pants.

When it comes to a fight, there's no honor. All that matters is that we survive, and our enemy is dead; we take nothing for granted.

Tia, Jake, and Theo spread out around the Minotaur, circling him. Buddy is raring to go, waiting for his master's command.

Alexandros and I stand in front of the Minotaur, with my sword ready in hand.

'We come in peace,' Theo tries to communicate as Alexandros snickers, not taking Theo seriously. But who would? No one says, 'We come in peace." We aren't talking to aliens.

The Minotaur roars again as a response, letting us know that he does not wish to communicate with his lunch. The Minotaur lunges towards Theo but misses as he jumps to the side.

Alexandros yells to Buddy to attack; the hound lunges towards the Minotaur. But amazingly, the pure power of the Minotaur just backhands Buddy as he smashes him into the Labyrinth wall, knocking him out.

The Minotaur turns and charges, but this time towards me, with its axe raised ready for a deadly blow. I hold my sword in hand, ready to block the mighty blow from the Minotaur; as it rushes towards me, time seems to slow down.

From the corner of my eye, I see a flaming arrow strike the Minotaur; it stumbles. I swing, slashing out against the axe, slicing it in half.

Roaring in anger, the Minotaur drops the remainder of the axe and picks up one of the stone pillars up over his head, aiming it at me.

I stand there, frozen, looking up at the stone pillar as it closes in on me.

But just before the pillar hits me, I am knocked away by a strong force of water, saving me seconds before being flattened.

I look up to see Tia standing there with water swirling around her hands. I mouth a 'thank you' before getting back up on my feet.

From the other side of the room, Theo continues to shoot arrows, each one hitting its mark, but only angering it even further, but at least keeping the beast occupied.

'Cut off it's horns!' yells Tia. 'It will make it weaker.'

Alexandros helps Theo occupy the Minotaur by creating dark sources to attack the beast.

'Hey!' I yell, catching the attention of the beast.

The Minotaur stops fighting the boys and turns to face me, charging me again. I don't think he likes me.

I steady myself.

The Minotaur, facing me with his head down, horns out as he gets closer.

I remember my training even though it was short. It feels like I've been doing it forever. I spring to the side and raise my sword. Just as its horns brush by my chest, I bring down the sword with as much force as I can, slicing the horns clean off its head as it crashes into the wall.

The Minotaur roars in rage as it stands up, staring me down. Simultaneously, Theo fires a barrage of arrows, Tia steps up from behind and thrusts her sword into its back, Alexandros creates a wave of darkness blinding the Minotaur, and I step up, slicing its chest open with my longsword.

The Minotaur bellows out in agony before collapsing motionless to the ground.

I let out a gasp of air, leaning over, hands on my legs, trying to catch my breath, not taking my eyes off the lifeless Minotaur.

'We did it!' I huff.

'Oh no! Where's Jake?' Tia asks.

I look over, and see him standing against the wall, quivering. Alexandros then runs towards Buddy; to our relief, we see him get back up on his legs, giving Alexandros a big sloppy lick, or should I say many licks.

CHAPTER 18

Another One?

'**W**ell done', says an unfamiliar voice from behind me.
Turning around, I am greeted by a young teenage boy with curly brown hair and matching brown eyes, his face still that of a child, as if he had still not grown out of his youthful features.

'Who are you?' I ask, stepping away from the boy.

'Why, me? Oh, no one important. But you, on the other hand, you're the ones from the prophecy,' he responds.

'What's your name, kid?' Theo asks.

'Luke.'

'Well, Luke, what are you doing in the middle of the Labyrinth?'

'On a quest.'

'A quest given to you by whom?'

The boy smirks before continuing, 'From Zorander himself.'

After receiving no response from us, Luke's smirk grows bigger. 'What? Not expecting to see one of Zorander's so soon?'

'Do you know who you're up against?' Alexandros asks, not fazed by the boy gloating in front of us.

'Oh, I'm not afraid. My father is the king of the gods.'

'Not possible,' I question.

'How not, my lady?' he says, sarcastically bowing down.

'Cut the cr*p because I, myself, am the daughter of Zeus.'

Luke's childish smile disappears as he acknowledges what I just said, staring at me emotionless.

As if remembering why he was here, he snaps back to his childish attitude.

'Hello, sister.'

I cannot believe it—I have a brother (half-brother). Maybe in another circumstance I will be jumping up and down with joy, but knowing that my brother is a follower of Zorander, I'm taken aback. Maybe it's too late to save him. But he is still blood.

'Unbelievable,' I respond.

'I guess we can see which child Zeus fancied the most, considering you were claimed by him and not left at an orphanage.'

'I was no—'

'Zorander warned me what you brainwashed demigods are like, believing that the gods actually care about you,' Luke argues, cutting me off.

'I've only met Zeus once, and that was two days ago, right after I received my prophecy. But that doesn't mean that he doesn't care about us,' I try to reason.

'I haven't seen my father, and I sure as hell don't want to see him!' Luke snaps, releasing all the emotions he has bottled up throughout the years. 'I was rescued by Zorander at the age of five from the orphanage in Athens. I'm now sixteen, and the only person who's cared about me is Zorander. He helped me figure out who my father was and helped me control the elements that came with being a child of the top three gods. He believed in me enough that he sent me on this quest alone . . . except I was told not to communicate with you, just spy, gain information, and then pass it back to him.'

'But you spoke to us. You had to have done it for a reason,' I ask.

'True. I wanted to see what the fuss was all about. You really don't seem like heroes.'

Tia steps closer to Luke. 'The hero works with a desire to protect others, a willingness to take on suffering if it keeps others safe. They develop the understanding, to do whatever it takes, if it's the right thing to do. Heroes work hard every day for others and consider it an honor to have the chance to do so . . . So don't you ever say that again.'

'You're on the wrong side, son,' agrees Jake; a blank expression is shared between the two boys.

'The man you look up to is a villain. His only desire is power and money. He thinks nothing of others... He's using you to overthrow Olympus, and once he has done that, he will throw you all away,' Tia adds.

'Very well said, but how can I believe anything you've said? We've just met?'

'Have you faced your fears?' I ask him. Luke does not reply. "Look around you, look on the floor. If Zorander really cared about you, he wouldn't have sent you to a place like this. If we were not here, you would have been dead,' I continue.

'Just because you've been given a prophecy doesn't mean you're stronger and greater than I am,' Luke says in anger as he lashes out towards me, dagger in hand.

I push him to the side. He turns back around, face full of anger.

'Sister, you really think that your kindness will save you?'

His eyes begin to turn gold, sparks of electricity swirl around the pupil. Before he can do any damage, Alexandros shouts a chant. "Παιδί ύπνου!" *Child Sleep!*

Silence fell throughout the whole Labyrinth as Luke drops onto the stone ground with a thump. A magical chant won't work on a beast as big as a Minotaur.

'That should hold him for a couple of hours,' Alexandros says, picking up his sleeping body.

CHAPTER 19

Alexandros's POV

Carrying Luke's sleepless body in my arms, we make our way towards the New York portal. We decided that it was better to keep him with us, even if that option did involve a kidnapping, making us no better than Zorander.

I guess you can call me an outsider, a lone wolf, but over time, I have learnt how to lessen the pain. I've learnt to hide my emotions, shield my heart from the world.

I still see the faces children make when they notice me at the sanctuary, the way they distance themselves when I get too close, as if being near them drained their happiness, all because I'm the son of Hades, god of the underworld.

I have gone as far as I can on this path alone. I've learnt how to cope with and solve my problems. What's left is a form of loneliness that requires happiness to solve.

Being different is not a bad thing. I was like no other demigod. I lived in the underworld with my father, Persephone, and the spirits that dwelt down below. I did visit the world above regularly to attend classes at the Olympic Sanctuary, but even at camp, I avoided everyone. It was safer that way.

I had no friends, but I don't blame them. I made no effort because then I didn't need to put my trust in anyone. It'll be safer, easier to choose not to stay. I have learnt that the only way one can be safe is to distance yourself from the world above. Just like my father, I prefer the underworld.

It took time, but I eventually found out what it meant being the son of Hades, and that made me stronger. I didn't let anyone in up until this prophecy. It changed everything for me, the idea of being involved in something bigger than myself, a chance of friendships, and maybe even love.

I admire Iris, everything about her, from the way the breeze blows through her long brown hair to the determination in her spirit. It wasn't just me who had a high opinion of her. She is, after all, the daughter of Zeus. She is unfailingly kind: she always put others first and herself last. Even though I've known her for a short few days, it's felt like a lifetime.

'The New York portal is right ahead,' Jake says as he points towards the mist ahead of us.

'Woof!' Buddy barks in agreement.

I dismiss Buddy back to the underworld before I address the others, 'Let's go.'

I step through the portal, facing my head down, as I try to shield my face from the bright sun. Blinking away the light, I can finally see New York.

'Central Park,' Iris gasps as she emerges from the mist, standing beside me.

She was, indeed, correct; we were in the middle of Central Park.

The park was beautiful, crossed by pathways so convenient that they might have been purposefully designed to lead from one centre to another. A slight breeze rustles the leaves, making them fall to the solid ground one by one. The air was warm, the beams of sunlight glowing on my skin. Flowers are vast, and they conceal the freshly-cut green grass. Flower hedges and bushes grew all around, making the park look more pleasant and attractive.

Dogs exercised with balls and Frisbees; families were having picnics and games of soccer. The bench directly beside me looks as if it had been exposed to the elements for many seasons, likely to be older than Zeus himself. It had come to resemble driftwood; the bright tones of its once-fresh state had become a somber brown.

'Where to now?' asks Theo, being the last to exit the Labyrinth.

The mortals aren't even fazed by us; as to them, they see nothing out of the norm.

'We need to travel to South Carolina,' replies Tia. 'This place is so beautiful,' she adds.

'That's more than half of a day's travel by car.' Jake sighs.

'There is an Olympic car rental in Virginia. So we just need to make it there, then we can drive the rest of the way to South Carolina,' Theo responds.

'We need to get from here to Washington by tonight, then tomorrow from there to Virginia. Then lastly, on the third day, to South Carolina.'

'It's about midday. If we split up and buy further supplies, that will last us for the three-day trip,' suggests Iris.

'And a map,' I contribute.

'Yes, and a map.'

'What are we going to do with the drooling kid?' asks Theo.

'I'll look after him,' Iris volunteers as she takes a seat on the wooden bench. 'Leave him here with me.'

'He will be out for another hour, just enough time for us to grab the essentials and make our way back here before he wakes,' I say, placing Luke on the bench beside her. He slumps over and leans his head on her shoulder, still fast asleep.

CHAPTER 20

Anastasia's POV

J ake and Alexandros went off towards Times Square, Luke and Iris stayed at Central Park, leaving Theo and I, to retrieve a map of South Carolina and New York City.

I am no stranger to prophecies. I had my first quest at sixteen, where two other demigods and I went on a quest to save a fellow centaur from the hands of Cyclopes. But this current one is, by far, the worst.

The fate of many lives lay in our hands; we must accomplish what the prophecy set out for us, the children of the strongest gods, together to protect the world from chaos.

Sounds *easy*.

I grew up in Kalamata, Southern Greece, where I lived in a house on the edge of the Nedon River, with my mother, stepdad, and younger half-brother.

Growing up, I lived an above-average life. Let us just say my family had no problems with money. I attended regular school, and during the summer school holidays, I spent the whole twelve weeks at the Olympic Sanctuary. There, I learnt how to fight, write, read in Ancient Greek and control my unique abilities.

At the sanctuary, I was not friends with Alexandros, Jake, or Theo. We all had our separate group of friends. Around camp, we did see each other, but we rarely spoke. The school life at the sanctuary wasn't really any different from the regular school I attended. We still had the popular group, outsiders, jocks, and nerds.

But the one thing the Olympic Sanctuary had that the mortal schools lacked was companionship and obviously mystical powers, or by what the mortals call it, *magic*. At the sanctuary, we would have one another's back, no matter who your godly parent was. In the end, we fought for one another, attend quests together, and experience things most teens would never accomplish in a lifetime.

At my mortal school, I was one of the girls you would envy. I was smart and sporty, and everyone gave me their undying attention, which resulted to everyone assuming I had the 'perfect' life. I would receive hurtful messages from girls who resented and envied me. But I tried to not let it get to me because they were unaware of how I really was deep down inside. I was alone. No one could know the truth about me. I had to lie about everything, so all my friendships were built up on a foundation of lies.

I used to wish that I could become 'normal,' be an average girl with the average struggles and high school problems, without always having to double-check my back.

Theo and I had finally reached a shopping mall deliberately designed for tourists, where you can find T-shirts, hats, magnets with huge logos of New York City all over it.

'Look what I found!' Theo says excitingly, showing off a map.

'Very funny . . . but this isn't it,' I respond, returning the map back on the stand.

'Want a shirt?' Theo asks, unfolding a shirt with 'I <3 New York' printed on it.

'Hard pass,' I say, crinkling up my nose.

After walking around the store for a few minutes, I come across the map we needed. 'Found it.'

I pay for it before heading out the store with Theo close behind.

'I'm starving. Do you want to grab something for lunch?' Theo suggests, rubbing his hand over his stomach, dramatically making a statement.

'I can't possibly turn down food.'

I follow Theo down the street where we find ourselves outside a small cafe, its royal blue paint glistening in the golden rays of the day.

Outside on the crowded street, hundreds of people rush by it. The half-a-dozen customers glance up as we enter the cafe. Unlike the outside, the interior of the cafe was warm and cheery, with bright lights and colorful walls. Waiters were smartly dressed in black and white, and the customers quickly return to their conversations as Theo and I take our seats in one of the vacant tables; our knees almost touching under the narrow table.

I remove my elbows from the table and sit a little straighter, grabbing one of the menus from our table, deciding on what to order.

'Ready to order?'

I look up from my menu, making eye contact with Theo before responding to the old waitress hovering over us. In her hand is a small writing pad. Theo orders a chicken burger and a strawberry milkshake, and I just order a grilled sandwich and an iced chocolate.

After engaging in small talk, our meals arrived shortly after; the filling of my sandwich had layers of cheese and ham with lettuce and tomato. Oozing from the sides was copious amounts of mayonnaise, feeling as if I needed to dislocate my jaw, just like a snake to eat it. After the well-deserved lunch, we return to Central Park, where the others were waiting for us.

'He's still out?' I ask, motioning towards Luke.

'Yeah . . .'

'Don't worry, he'll be up soon,' Alexandros assures us.

'Did you guys find a map?' he asks.

'Yep,' I say, showing off the map Theo and I retrieved.

'Uhm, just had a funny thought. But like, couldn't you guys have just used "Olympic Search" *(Google Search for you, mere mortals)* on your smartphones?' Jake says.

'Old fashion is the way to go,' Theo responds.

'Great! Now this may seem strange, but Alexandros and I discovered something you'd like to hear,' Jake mentions.

'We think we may need to go to Central Park Zoo,' he suggests.

'Why?'

'We may be in luck, I think I found us transportation to Washington DC,' Alexandros adds.

'I don't know if I'm going to like where this is going,' mutters Theo, catching onto the idea.

Alexandros shows off one of his evil smirks. 'You won't believe us even if we tell you.'

'Out with it!' Iris snaps impatiently.

'Nah-uh, you're going to have to trust us.'

CHAPTER 21

Fly Away

A weight releases off my shoulder. Moving my hand, I massage the numbness away.

Quickly realising what just occurred, I turn to see Luke yawning, wiping the sleep from his eyes.

He is awake.

'Morning, sunshine,' Alexandros says as he leans on his thighs, looking at Luke, making sure the spell has worn off.

Startled, Luke jumps backwards off the bench.

'What happened? Where am I? Someone answer me! Wait . . . Did you kidnap me? Just you wait until Zorander finds out!'

'You done?' Alexandros interrupts, having enough of Luke's complaining.

'Yes . . . No—'

'Take a deep breath . . . try to calm down,' Alexandros tells him, trying to reassure that everything is fine.

'I can't be out here . . .,' he finally lets out.

'What do you mean?' asks Tia.

'Zorander has forbidden us from stepping foot out in the mortal world,' he says, nerves beginning to show.

'Well, sorry to break it to you, kid, but you've broken two of his rules already,' Theo chimes in.

Luke, realising what he has done and that Zorander will be deeply upset with him, begins to worry.

'He's going to . . .,' Luke begins to whimper; tears begin to form in his eyes.

I do not wish to know what Zorander has promised the demigods if they ever cross paths with him or disobey his orders.

'Hey, no, if you stay with us, he won't hurt you.'

He looks up at me. The next thing he does shocks everyone, including me.

Walking up to me slowly and hesitantly, he reaches out and *hugs* me.

Realising what's happened, and once the shock wore off, I lean down, hugging him back. His body trembles as he begins to cry.

'Shh, it's going to be okay,' I whisper, not letting him go.

Luke pulls away, wiping his tears away with the sleeve of his shirt.

'You're part of the team now,' Alexandros says as he awkwardly pats him on the shoulder. Luke smiles up at him. 'He won't lay a hand on you.'

Even though Alexandros means well, how can we trust him? Suddenly, he's on our side when he's spent all these years with Zorander.

It just doesn't add up.

'I'd hate to rush things, but we need to head to Central Park Zoo,' reminds Jake.

Picking up our backpacks, we head towards the zoo. My stomach grumbles, and I wonder why Tia and Theo aren't hungry.

The zoo was a lively place with its large display of animals and birds of different species. We made our way towards the ticket box, where we were greeted by a young male. With a formal statement of greeting and withered lips casting a genuine smile, he hands us the tickets.

Everyone was enjoying the zoo, except the animals, the animals that were forced to live in enclosed habitats.

'The zoo's map shows that it's directly up ahead,' Jake shows Alexandros as they have their secret conversation, not indulging the rest of us.

'Nearly there,' Alexandros states without a glance towards us.

We follow Alexandros through the zoo as he leads us to whatever creature they were whispering about.

'You sure you're going the right way?' I ask as Alexandros and Jake lead us into a deserted section of the zoo.

'Just the right place,' he responds.

We stand there for what seems like a microsecond before we are greeted by a middle-aged lady, who seemed to have appeared out of nowhere.

'Ready to see the real wonders of the zoo?' she asks in a sweet humming voice.

'Welcome to Artemis's sacred animal enclosure,' she says as she leads us through a gate that wasn't there a few seconds ago.

Artemis is the goddess of wild animals, the hunt, wilderness, childbirth, and virginity. We share the same father—Zeus.

Walking through the mystical gate, a new part of the zoo opened.

Instead of your average zoo animals, this new section of the zoo was made up with mythical creatures.

To my left, a huge water enclosure; inside, a few hippocampus swim around playfully. A hippocampus is a fish-tailed horse of the sea, with head and foreparts of a horse and the serpentine tail of a fish.

The enclosure beside the hippocampus was open, with a creature that has the body, tail, and back legs of a lion and the head and wings of an eagle—*a griffin.*

This mythical zoo had chimeras, harpies, and various mythical creatures in many different sizes.

I look around wide-eyed. This is unbelievable. Who would have guessed that 'mythical' creatures would be disguised inside a regular zoo?

Jake walks in line with the lady, talking to her before she smiles and nods. 'This way,' she motions to him.

We all follow closely behind.

Leading us into a huge open paddock, she motions towards the creatures roaming the meadows.

'No way!' Tia gasps in excitement.

A couple dozen majestic-winged horses roam around in the paddock ahead of us.

'These are the offspring of Pegasus himself,' the lady explains.

Pegasus is the offspring of the Olympian god Poseidon and gorgon Medusa. He was said to be pure white; he would help demigods on their quests and save wounded soldiers in battle. But now it is said that he is stabled by Zeus and tasked with drawing the chariot of his thunderbolts. Even though Pegasus was pure white, his offspring varied in color.

Unlike the natural herds of the forest, these horses were every color, shape, and size. The only thing each had in common was the halter it wore on its head for an easy capture.

'This was your grand idea?' Theo huffs at the sight of the winged horses.

'It's great, right?' Jake replies, not picking up on the sarcasm.

'Yeah, that's definitely the word for it . . .'

'So, we're riding those?' I ask.

'Yes, and as demigods, they will assist you to Washington DC, but they will not go any further,' the lady confirms.

'That's all we ask of them,' responds Alexandros.

'Come on, I'll introduce you.' The lady leads us into the open paddock. 'Now let them choose you.'

One of the horses excludes itself from the group, making its way towards me. It was golden white in color, its mane long and wavy, almost hiding the large golden eye beneath it. Out of nowhere, it spreads two feathery wings; the span must have been over a couple of metres long.

CHAPTER 22

Alexandros's POV

We were chosen one by one, all except me. Maybe the dark aroma that drifts around me is frightening off the pegasi.

Then out of nowhere, thundering hooves split the silence around me as a lone stallion gallops through the barren landscape, the wind whipping his mane through the air, its muscles ripple from under his torso and powerful legs, propelling him forward as he powers over towards me. Slowing down just in time before it reaches me, it neighs approvingly as I rub its neck.

We thank the lady before mounting the pegasi.

The gust of forced air flattens the surrounding area. Then the Pegasus charges forward at full gallop. In seconds, we were airborne, its legs tuck up underneath, safe, out of sight, like the undercarriage of a plane.

He glides on above the tall New York skyscrapers, and on toward Washington DC, he began to gain height. As the wind tousled the Pegasus's mane and whipped it about as we flew over America, I could feel the heat of the summer sun beating down on my back; the leather reins rubbing against my fingers, soon to be blisters.

As a child, I used to wake up in the middle of the night and wish for the sun. The darkness taunted me; my imagination supplied many beasts with horrifying jaws, eyes, and voices that lurk beyond the range of my vision. We all have demons we try to fight and forget. With the help of my father, I learnt to embrace mine.

My biological mother died during childbirth, and Hades didn't want his only son to grow up as an orphan, so I was brought down to the underworld.

Living and being brought up in the underworld really takes a toll on a child, being surrounded by monsters, lost souls, the dead, and the only light coming from the fire within the darkness. But I had my father there to help me through it step by step. Once I had obtained the age of eight, I was allowed up to the surface to attend some lessons at the Olympic Sanctuary. I did not have friends up there. I felt like an outcast, and that made it incredibly hard to fit in, being the only child of a god that lived amongst their godly parent. They envied me, but at the same time, they were terrified of me because of who I am.

I know the ins and outs of the underworld as I watched each soul that passed through to judgement. There are two entrances to the underworld that the dead pass through once they have been escorted there by psychopomp, creatures of Hades: Pluto's gate and the River Styx. Once you pass through these entrances, you will need to pay Charon, the spirit of the dead, three drachmas to cross the Acheron. Once they've made it this far, they will need to walk a cold and chilling road until they come to the seated Aeacus, Minos, and Rhadamanthys—the sons of Zeus who judge the souls of the diseased; they sit in front of Hades's palace. Aeacus judges those who came from Europe, whilst Rhadamanthys judges those from Asia. Minos, on the other hand, would only decide if Aeacus or Rhadamanthys were indecisive.

Once the deceased have been judged, they are either sent to three locations for the rest of eternity. But each place depends on your life as a human. The first place is known as the Elysium Fields, the paradise to which heroes whom the gods conferred immortality to were sent. It's a land of perfect happiness. You must live a righteous life to be granted entry. The second place was the Fields of Asphodel, a section within the underworld where indifferent and ordinary souls who lived a life of neither good nor evil were sent to live after death. Majority of the mortal souls are sent to live here after judgement. The last and most horrifying place to end up is Tartarus, the place where people who were evil during their lives face eternal punishment. I can still hear their screams as they were being tortured by the furies.

My father had Cerberus, the hound of Hades, to guard his domain at the gates of hell from the unwanted. He is Bud's father, except Bud did not take his ghastly features. Cerberus had a mane of snakes, three dog heads, a serpent's tail, and claws of a lion. A truly deadly beast, its slobber from the heads were poisonous.

Hades was the firstborn of the Titans Cronus and Rhea. You may also know Hades by the name of Pluto and Pluton. The Ancient Greeks have been depicting Hades as a stern, pitiless god, who was unmoved by prayer or sacrifice, making him the most feared, hated, and misunderstood god of all time. This is all a whole load of nonsense; my father is none of that. Demigods have been brought up to fear Hades, and when they think of him, all they see is the underworld, darkness, and death. But the thing is my father is more than his job. He is loving, loyal, and would always be there for me when I needed him.

Also, the story of my father being a kidnapper is completely wrong. He did not kidnap Persephone. He was struck by her beauty and tenderness that he fell in love with her. So instead of abducting her, *which is commonly believed*, Persephone willingly came to the underworld and married Hades. Also, all the dark and gory punishments given to the sinners of Tartarus, well, Persephone is behind it all, not my father. Her name means 'chaos bringer,' and she takes it quite literally, although she is a loving stepmum.

Almost all the troubles plaguing the Greek gods can be traced back to Zeus. Not my father. Hades is a good and just ruler. He didn't impregnate people he wasn't supposed to. *Zeus, I may or may not be referring to you.* He didn't start wars for no reason and condemn people for eternal punishment, which is something Zeus would do for fun. Thank the gods, Zeus can't read my mind. Otherwise, I'd be struck by lightning for speaking ill about the 'king of the gods.'

Loyalty to the gods meant never questioning their motives. The gods in Ancient Greece often send tests to citizens, and if they maintained faith through the tests, it was a sign of their loyalty and belief. This is how you'd know where you stand amongst the Olympian gods. The gods have many human qualities as they constantly fought with one another, behaved irrationally and unfairly, and were often jealous of one another.

Zeus was the last child of the Titans Cronus and Rhea; he was often referred to as the god of thunder. He dispensed justice and was very, *very* strict and harsh with his punishments. *Trust me, you don't want to be on his bad side.* He often cheated on his wife, Hera, by sleeping with anyone who took his fancy—I mean, *anyone.* He has also fathered many iconic heroes, namely Hercules, Minos, Polydeuces, Arcas, Zethus, and Perseus. Zeus used any means necessary to get what he wanted, but even after all these harsh things I've said about him, he is still an excellent ruler—wise, fair, just, merciful, and prudent.

Poseidon was the second son of the Titans Cronus and Rhea. He's the god of the sea, earthquakes, storms, and horses. His nickname is Earth Shaker because he creates earthquakes when he's in a bad mood. His iconic symbol is the three-pronged trident that he always carries around. Being protector of the seas, he lives on the ocean floor, in a palace made of coral and gems. Through his life, Poseidon has started many fights; one of the ones you may know is the fight for Athens against Athena. A contest took place in the Acropolis to see who would gain the power over Athens. Poseidon struck a boulder with his trident and produced a horse. Athena brought forth an olive tree from the earth by the touch of her spear. He lost the war and the city to Athena.

Poseidon also designed and created all the creatures of the sea. As god of earthquakes, Poseidon is also connected to dry land, and many of his places of worship in Greece were inland, but these temples were centered on pools and streams of water. One of his well-known temples is located in Attica, Greece.

Apollo is the twin of Artemis, son of Zeus and the Titan Leto. Apollo is the god of the sun, prophecies, healing, arts, archery, and poetry. He was also gifted the power to see the future and heal or give people illnesses. He is known as a masterful magician, who would delight Olympus with his tunes played on his golden lyre. His lyre is a stringed instrument that resembles a small harp; the god Hermes created the instrument. Apollo taught men the art of medicine, so he was often referred to as the healer.

Demigods are far stronger than humans; the children of the big three are even stronger than the normal demigods. All demigods can heal faster than humans, have higher stamina, above-average strength that can keep us alive during a fight—*all the plus sides of being half-god, half-human.*

Here, I will break up the abilities each demigod has over their godly parents' domain. I'll only mention our abilities because we don't want to be here forever.

The children of Apollo are superior archers, healers, and musicians. Only some rare few have the ability to control fire and light, Theo being one of the rare few. He can also produce an extremely-high-pitch whistle as an attack during battle. He can also afflict others with curses through poetry.

Children of Zeus are known to have control over the domain of heaven, also known to possess great bravery and strength. They also have control over electrokinesis and aerokinesis. Electrokinesis can be used to control electricity and being able to withstand powerful electric shocks. They can also summon lightning bolts. Aerokinesis can be used to control air and even fly with practice.

The children of Poseidon have the power over Poseidon's domain with capacity to generate earthquakes and hurricanes, able to control and create water without being near a water source. They can also communicate telepathically with equine and sea creatures since Poseidon created them.

Children of Hephaestus, i.e., Jake, are greatly skilled builders and craftsmen. Their talent as fabricators are second to none. They can operate and improve any piece of machinery, in a short period of time; that's why we have him here with us for the *Argo*. In extremely rare cases, they are blessed with the ability to create and control fire.

Lastly, me, a son of Hades, I have control over his subjects in his kingdom beneath the earth. I can also summon earthquakes, just like Poseidon's children. Last but not least, I can control and *raise* the dead.

CHAPTER 23

Anastasia's POV

T he pegasi fly high above Washington DC.

It was late in the afternoon.

As we flew over the Washington Monument, the towering tribute to George Washington made up of marble, granite, and bluestone gneiss, which happens to be the world's tallest predominantly stone structure.

The pegasi dropped us off at West Potomac Park but not before Alexandros sent of a gust of mist, shielding the human eyes of our arrival.

We head towards the hotel that Jake booked for us through his smartphone during our flight.

There are many secret businesses run by demigods that we can use as protection during our travels; this hotel was one of those places.

The streets of Washington DC were glorious in its inception. The sidewalks were smooth grey stones joined with such precision that the joints were almost invisible.

We arrive at the Shoreline Hotel. The walls were concrete but not like a villa in rural Greece; they were more akin to the construction of a modern skyscraper, all sharp edges and corners. The hotel was luxurious, with its waterfront views.

We check in to the hotel, receiving a luxurious suite. The hotel windows overlook the Pentagon across the lagoon.

The Pentagon is the headquarters of the United States Department of Defense, also known as the world's largest office building.

The room is bathed with natural light, unrivalled views of the Potomac River, a grand staircase from the thirteenth and fourteenth floor, king-sized beds in three separate rooms, as well as a fold-out sofa bed. The wraparound balcony in the main room lets us view Washington whilst safe within the walls of the building.

'Wow, I could stay here forever!' Iris exclaims as she falls dramatically on the couch that lay in the middle of the suite.

'This place calls me poor in so many different ways . . .,' adds Theo.

'Dinner is at seven, reservations at the Shakers Lodge, dress appropriately,' Jake says, checking his schedule on the smartphone.

'We'd be lost without you,' jokes Alexandros.

'Tia and I dibs the main bedroom on the fourteenth floor!' shouts Iris as she rushes upstairs.

'Hell yeah!' I say as I join her up the stairs to change for dinner.

The bedroom closet was filled with many styles of fancy dresses to casual attire.

'What about this one?' Iris asks as she shows me a short black mini dress.

'I'm not feeling it.'

'This one?' She shows a dark-blue jumpsuit.

'I feel that gives off a plumber outfit vibe.'

'Not wrong,' Iris says with a giggle.

After having a quick but thoughtful shower, I blow-dry my hair without brushing it. I would rather not look like a fuzzy mess. I change into the dress I chose for this evening's dinner.

I shroud my body in the long and loose baby blue gown made of soft satin fabric. I would have preferred the bright-red dress, but this was not the right occasion for it.

Iris joins me in the bedroom; she walks as lightly as an acrobat, wearing a mango-colored skirt and a crème top made of silk like materials, the silk skirt peppering her body with soft, sensual kisses.

'That dress looks lovely on you,' she complements as soon as she notices me.

'Thank you, as do you.'

'Come on, the boys are waiting for us,' she says, grabbing a pair of skin-colored heels and retreating down the stairs with me closely behind.

Making our way downstairs where we are greeted by the boys, I connect eyes with Theo, his face in awe as he stares at me. He didn't need to say anything, for it was written on his face.

He stood there, proud, aware of his own looks. He was like the sun, he had people orbiting around him at camp. He was one of those well-known boys' teenage girls would constantly drool over. In one way or another, all the people who met him felt attracted to him. He was the brightest person you could ever meet—no pun intended.

'Ladies, you look dashing,' Luke says as he bows before us, hand outstretched.

'Thank you, as do you, young sir,' Iris responds, taking his hand.

Alexandros was wearing his signature look—dark leather jacket, white button-up shirt, and leather Dr. Martens. Theo was looking very vintage in a charcoal wool overcoat and grey chino pants. Jake was wearing a dark-blue polo shirt and crème dress shorts. And Luke was wearing a long grey knit jumper and blue chino pants.

The street leading towards the Shakers Lodge, once sleek with tarmac, now greyed by the bleaching of the sun; the streetlamps, once painted in glossy blue, now dapple with grey chips of undercoat.

The lighting was dim inside the restaurant, and the air was thick with the aroma of so many different foods. I knew the food was going to be expensive by the way the waiter looks down his nose at us and sneered when he spoke. Only in the most upper-class restaurants did the waiters have an attitude like that. I feel the eyes of other patrons follow us as we were escorted to a table for six.

I observe the restaurant, and what caught my eyes were the waiters, their black uniforms neatly ironed and tucked in, with white ties around their necks.

I peruse the wine list. 'Cough' 'What?' I turn my attention towards Theo. 'We're eighteen.' 'So?' 'We're in the United States of America, you have to be twenty-one and over to consume alcohol' 'Ugh' I grumble, as I return the wine list to the table, retrieving the food menu, scouting for the most expensive meal, a smirk appearing on my face. Eating here was going to cost the Olympic Sanctuary an arm and a leg. *We demigods were treated with luxury during quests. We were lucky enough to receive a platinum card to spend as we like.* Yay *to us!*

As we wait for our food, I listen to the noisy chatter of all the people sitting around me. The restaurant is large; outside the windows, I can see the sunset in the horizon, rich hues of red blended with oranges.

As our meals are distributed amongst us, we discuss the ongoing adventure without gaining a single mortal's attention.

I excuse myself from the others as I go and use the restroom—perfumed air, stainless steel shiny taps, hot hand dryer, self-flush toilets, and piped music.

I wash my hands, drying them under the blow dryer.

I look myself in the mirror, reapplying gloss on my plump lips. 'Creek.'

I snap my head towards the noise, but no one was there.

'Hello?' I ask, looking around the restroom, on edge.

'Quark!'

I drop my lip gloss.

'Coo, coo' I must be dreaming, she's cooing like a bird.

The noise comes directly behind me; there stood an old lady.

Did she just 'quark' at me?

'Can I help you?'

The old woman wore a dark frayed robe, with a hood that hid her bird-like facial features, making her look more like a vulture than a person.

'You! You!' I swear she just cawed.

Startled, I step backwards, trying to distance myself from the crazy old lady.

She begins to shriek, uttering in ecstatic frenzy.

'You are the cause of many deaths,' she continues. 'You will cause the death of someone of value. Because of you, people will perish.' Her voice gave that of a yapping sound.

There were more insults as I hurried past her, trembling. I ran through the bathroom doors, right into Theo's arms.

'What? Are you okay? What happened?' he asks, startled.

'There—' I stop. I am causing a scene. Taking a deep breath, I continue, 'Nothing . . . just a spider.' I lie as I walk back to the others, hoping Theo would believe me and return with me.

Dinner finishes not long after, and we return to the hotel room.

The others retreat to their sleeping quarters, leaving me standing alone in the kitchen. As I grab a glass of water, memories of the old lady's encounter return, and I shudder.

'You okay?' I turn to see Theo. Having the same idea as I, grabbing a glass of water.

'Yeah . . .'

He looks at me intensely, as if trying to read my thoughts.

As if pleased with what he learnt, he smiles. 'Lies.' He takes a sip from his glass. 'I can tell when you're lying. What happened earlier?'

I stand there contemplating whether to tell him the truth. But my heart failed me, 'There was a creepy old lady in the washroom with me, she-she appeared out of nowhere, throwing horrific chants at me.' I give in.

Staring, deep in thought, he finally responds, 'By any chance, did she sound like a bird when she chanted her taunts?'

I nod.

'Sibyl.'

'A what?' I ask.

'She was a sibyl, an Ancient Greek Delphic oracle, similar to the oracle of Delphi, but when she gives a prophecy, she's never wrong.' He pushes, 'What did she say?'

'Just that I will be the cause of a lot of death.' I did not wish to include the death of someone of value to me, whatever did that mean.

'Doesn't take a lot of common sense to know that's an outcome of a quest,' he huffs.

He washes my glass and his own before telling me there was nothing to worry about and sending me off to bed.

I lay in bed, pensive about everything, until I am buried in sleep.

CHAPTER 24

Be Watchful

I wake to soft sheets, streaks of sunlight penetrate the window and blind me. Shedding myself from the remaining glimpses of a dream, the saddest part, is that, eventually, the memory of my dream will fade away. I stretch my arms above my head and yawn. I watch my legs dangle above the white carpet.

Anastasia is still sleeping peacefully in the bed beside me. I drag myself out of bed, being careful not to wake her. After showering and readying myself for the day, I change into jeans and white V-neck top.

I make my way downstairs, where I see Alexandros in the kitchen, brewing himself coffee.

'Morning.'

'Morning. You're up early,' he says, turning to face me. 'Want some coffee?'

'Yes, thank you.'

I take a seat at one of the stools around the kitchen counter, flipping through a magazine and looking through the glossy pages.

'Here.'

My eyes rest on the coffee mug. I reach out, retrieving it from him.

'Thank you,' I respond, taking a sip from the freshly-made coffee.

A few silent moments pass by before Alexandros breaks it.

'I need to ask you something,' he whispers, loud enough so only I can hear.

I raise an eyebrow. 'What about?'

He looks around, making sure no one was awake or nearby. 'I've been having a bad feeling about Jake—and no, before you say it, it has nothing to do with jealousy over his crafty skills. I just find it suspicious that Luke managed to find us in the Labyrinth all by himself, whilst we needed Bud to lead us through it.'

He was not wrong; how could he have found us?

'I didn't think of that before . . .'

'And the son of Zeus? I have a hard time believing Zorander would willingly let a child of Zeus wonder alone.'

He has a logical point.

'He's only sixteen. You saw how he—'

Alexandros interrupts me. 'You don't possibly believe him. That was all for show. He was so quick to side with us. No need for persuasion.' He continues, 'Jake came on our quest. Doesn't that raise enough questions in itself?'

I have a strange feeling about this, but somehow I believed Alexandros. A demigod would not risk everything for a quest they were not even prophesied for.

This quest involved lost demigods; it was far from safe.

'What do we do?' I ask.

'I don't know . . . Just be—' He stops midsentence as he makes eye contact with someone directly behind me.

'Morning,' Luke interrupts as he waddles through the kitchen, still half asleep.

'You look like cr*p, mate,' Alexandros says, changing the topic.

'Thanks . . .,' he mumbles.

'I'm in the mood for pancakes,' Luke suggests as he opens the fridge, pouring himself a glass of orange juice.

A few moments later, after finishing my coffee, I serve Luke breakfast—pancakes with fresh blueberries.

Soon afterwards, the others had woken up and joined us in the kitchen.

The moment the others slide into a chair, I serve them an enormous platter of food—eggs, ham, and a glass of orange juice.

Not long after, we pack our bags and head towards the Jones Point Lighthouse, waiting for the river ferry to take us down the Potomac River.

An old-fashioned boat docks at the edge of the water. We line up before boarding on to the ferry.

I take a seat next to Tia, opposite us sat Luke and Alexandros, as the ferry chugs forward towards our destination.

He is not usually the kind of guy I fantasise about. For starters, he's brunette, and I've always had a thing for blonds. I look for blue-eyed men with a handle on the world, a perfect description of Jake. But that changed as soon as I met Alexandros.

I watch him as he looks out the window, watching the waves crash against the side of the ferry. He doesn't notice me, so I gaze freely. There is something about him, a slight confidence and inflated ego, that has me struck like this.

Feeling my eyes on him, he turns and smiles. I feel my cheeks heating up, I quickly look away, avoiding his eye contact. Busted.

For the rest of the boat ride, I indulged myself with conversation.

The horn of the ferry toots twice, letting us know we had arrived at our destination—Stafford, Virginia.

Walking towards the bus stop, we walk past a whole crowd of people, each person moving as if unseeing hands drag them this way and that, each with a separate goal they need to achieve for the day.

I stand in the never-ending queue for the local bus. After a couple of minutes, the half-full bus arrives, stopping with a jerk.

I take a seat in one of the empty seats next to the window.

I turn to see someone had decided to sit next to me—Alexandros.

'I'm already over all this travelling,' he complains as he makes himself comfortable for the one-hour bus trip.

'We've got another full day of it.' I roll my eyes at the thought of the exhausting travel ahead.

The doors close with a gasp of air as the bus crawls forward.

The air conditioning, struggling to pump through the few filters, placed inconveniently around the bus, whistling with the extreme pressure to keep us cool.

Repeating its eternal patterns of stops and goes, going all sorts of directions and taking turns, failing to avoid the potholes and curbs.

'Did you hear what Jake said?' he asks, turning to face me.

'No.'

'He thinks we won't be able to stay within the city centre of Virginia, believes the scent of monsters are too strong,' he says without breaking eye contact.

'Isn't that rare to have a significant number of creatures within the city centre?' I didn't know much about these mystical Greek monsters.

'Yes, correct, but we aren't in Greece anymore. The monsters can go as they please. The mist still protects the human eyes from them, but they tend to surround densely-populated cities overseas, in case they catch a wondering demigod for dinner.'

The monsters don't attack regular humans. It's against everything they stand for. Trust me, they don't stand for much. However, this was one of their rules, they only prey on demigods and nymphs.

'Well, isn't that . . . great?'

'So where will we spend the night?' I ask.

'Shenandoah National Park.'

'So basically, the middle of nowhere.' I sigh.

'Yep, sounds fun!' he says with a sarcastic smile.

I turn my attention to the window, the greenery outside becomes a hazy blur, itching for the destination that will come eventually.

CHAPTER 25

Alexandros's POV

It was told that in Ancient Greece, the Greeks were perused by the gods disguised as animals. But I've learnt that an animal will always look away when you stare at it, dropping its eyes first, because it is believed that humans are the top of the food chain. But if it were a god in disguise, it will keep eye contact with you.

Gods were very fond of doing this, but this doesn't happen anymore—that we know of. Ladies and gents, be careful.

Even the demigods in Ancient Greece looked different from how we do now. Back then, it was easier to figure out who was a demigod and who was a mere mortal.

We demigods have gold blood, ichor running through our veins, or some like to say, '*the golden blood of the gods.*' But not in color, in essence. It used to affect our appearance; the Ancient Greek demigods looked disbelieving, with their golden hair, skin, and eyes that practically glowed. This was also a plus side for the gods, so that they did not start a war by accidentally killing the child of another god.

But now only a rare few of us may have those aspects. With the majority of the mortals no longer believing in the gods, we had to adapt, begin to look like them, making it incredibly difficult to stand out.

I had known Anastasia, Jake, and Theo from the sanctuary. I never really spoke to them. I kept to myself. But the first time I met Iris was at Mount Olympus. Where had the gods been hiding her?

When I walked into the throne room, my whole world slowed down. She was the most beautiful girl I had ever seen. With her Greek looks, tall frame, and high cheek bones, how can one not be mesmerised by her beauty? Her cheeks, the color of pink roses, and long eyelashes that frame her chocolate brown eyes. Her muscle definition was perfect, and she stood there with confidence. She was the kind of girl that women loved to hate. I knew from then that she was the girl who would change the way I looked at life.

The bus pulls in at Richmond, we make our way off the bus.

'The Olympian car hire is just up ahead,' mentions Jake, his eyes never leaving his smartphone.

'Can we get food first? I'm hungry,' Luke complains.

'Do you ever stop eating?' Theo asks.

'I'm a growing boy.'

'Sure, there's a food court up ahead,' Jake replies as he leads us towards the destination.

I look back to see Iris walking behind. I slow my pace so that I fall in line with her.

Her emotions were not easily hidden on her innocent face. Her pain was evident in the crease of her brow and forehead. As I look into her eyes, I knew something was wrong.

'Are you okay?'

She suddenly stops, grabbing my arm for balance. I reach out to hold her steady.

'Can't-can't you feel it?' she manages to let out.

I look around, trying to fathom what she's on about. 'No, what is it?'

'I feel very lightheaded,' she says, regaining her posture, rubbing her temples with the palm of her hands.

She looks star-struck at something to her left, 'You can't see that?' She points towards the emptiness.

'I can't see or feel anything. There's nothing there.'

'Guys, you good?' Tia asks as she notices we are no longer behind them.

'I don't think so,' I respond.

'Your hands!' Tia points towards Iris's hands.

Indeed there was something surreal happening to her hands, they were glowing bright yellow. I step back, putting distancing between us.

You do not want to be anywhere near an unstable demigod.

'You've just received your powers!' Luke shouts, running back towards her.

'What—?'

'Electrokinetic,' he cuts her off. 'You can now control electricity. Weird, though, because I got that ability at thirteen,' he boasts. 'Wow!' she manages to let out as she brings her hands in front of her face, admiring the sparkles of light.

'Test it out,' says Luke.

I now stare at Iris with utter fascination; waiting to see what she can do, to see if she can do anything at all. She turns to me, her face shone just like her hands, her veins glowing golden. She was the most astonishing girl I had ever met.

There was no one around. 'Give it a shot,' I suggest.

She extends her hands forward, her face straining under the pressure. Looking at her hands, all I can see is a few little sparks before she gives up disappointingly.

'Well, that was sad,' laughs Theo.

'Don't worry, it's full power will take time. Your body is charging just like a phone battery,' comforts Luke.

Her hands return to normal, and soon after, we reach the food court. The food is simple, and the decor is plain, filled with loud chatter, people raising their voices to be heard above the noise.

Luke and Jake walk off, grabbing meals for themselves.

I take a seat at one of the empty tables, the others doing the same.

Off in the distance, visible enough to be seen, a man in a blue hoodie sits staring right at us.

Sitting opposite me, I nudge Iris under the table.

Still off in her own world, I nudge her leg a bit harder.

'Ow! What was that for?!' She glares at me.

I roll my eyes at her. Ignoring the question, I reply, 'Turn around, don't make it obvious, but look behind you, at the man in a blue sports hoodie.'

She turns around, trying not to be obvious.

Turning back to me, she says, 'He is staring at us.'

'That's my point . . .,' I say, looking away from the strange man. 'What's his problem?'

I look back, and he was gone, vanished into thin air.

'He's gone,' I say, looking around the food court for him.

Iris turns looking at the now-empty location of the suspicious man.

'He got bored.' She shrugs it off.

Jake and Luke return to our table with their meals in hand.

'I'm so hungry,' Luke says as he bites into his food.

Once they had finished their meals, we headed towards the Olympian car hire.

The entrance to the car hire was bland, just a rustic sign to confirm you have arrived at your destination.

The area was enclosed by a high brick wall with razor wire. The two metal gates hung open. Directly ahead lay a shed with a security window, and beyond it, piles of cars, ranging from sports to luxurious cars, to your standard everyday car.

A middle-aged lady in a bright yellow vest, with the word STAFF written in bold, welcomes us.

'Afternoon. How can I help?' she asks.

'We were wondering if you can assist us. We're looking to hire a car,' Jake responds with our obvious intentions.

'What quest are you guys on?'

'Straight to the point,' Theo whispers.

The lady smiles and asks the question again.

'The most recent prophecy. We're the children of Zeus, Hades, Poseidon, and Apollo,' Tia answers the lady.

'And the most important, Hephaestus,' Jake includes himself with a bow.

Ignoring him, the lady continues, 'Here.'

She leads us towards what I think must be the most luxurious car in the car yard. I am unsure if that's a good or a bad thing.

'No way! Is that a BMW X7?!' Theo gasps, obviously intrigued by the pearl white car. 'I dibs driving.'

The lady hands us over the keys with no hesitation. With that, we drove out of the car yard and towards our destination for the night: *Shenandoah National Park.*

CHAPTER 26

Anastasia's POV

After my encounter with the sibyl, I have not been able to think about anything else.

Whose death was I accountable for? Was it someone here?

Theo informed me about the fate of the Cumaean Sibyl, who crossed paths with Apollo and was doomed to live for generations until only her voice remained—another example of what happens if you cross paths with an Olympian god.

But like us humans, the gods have their fate spun by the three sisters of fate—the Moirae—Lachesis, Clotho, and Atropos. No god or human have the power to influence or question their judgement.

Clotho, the youngest sister, spins the thread of life. Lachesis, the second sister, allocates the fate during the person's life. She measures the thread of life with her rod, determining the length and nature of the person's lifespan. The eldest sister, Atropos, is the cutter of the thread. She determines how someone will die and when.

The demigods of Ancient Greece did not have it as easy as us, such as Hercules, the son of Zeus and Alcmene. The legend goes that Hera (Zeus's wife) hated Hercules and wanted to kill him. He then was driven mad by Hera, killed his own sons whom he had with his wife Megara. After realising what he had done, he fled and went to the Oracle of Apollo, *the very same oracle that gave us our prophecy.* The oracle then commanded him to go to Tiryns and serve his cousin, King Eurystheus, for twelve years. Hercules's cousin loathed him, sending him to complete twelve impossible quests; they were

1. *Slay the Nemean Lion,*
2. *Slay the nine-headed Lernaean Hydra,*
3. *Capture the golden hind of Artemis,*
4. *Capture the Erymanthian boar,*
5. *Clean the Augean (the cannibal horses) stables in a single day,*
6. *Slay the Stymphalian birds,*
7. *Capture the Cretan bull,*
8. *Steal the mares of Diomedes,*
9. *Obtain the girdle of Hippolyta, queen of the Amazons,*
10. *Obtain the cattle of the monster Geryon,*
11. *Steal three golden apples of the Hesperides, and*
12. *Capture and bring back Cerberus (Hades's hound).*

Hercules managed to complete the twelve labors and free himself from the service of his cousin, now that was considered a 'happy ending'. If you were not lucky, you could end up like Atlas, the son of the Titan Iapetus and the Oceanid Clymene. Atlas supports the pillars that hold heaven and earth apart for eternity, condemned by Zeus as punishment for leading the Titans in their battle against the Olympian gods for control of Mount Olympus.

After an hour drive from the car hire, we had reached Shenandoah National Park.

After parking the car, we began our journey to the top of one of the mountains and into the next valley, the safest point for us to spend the night.

The wilderness hums with life all around me. I twirl about, gazing up at the canopy. The sun breaks through the trees, lighting up the dirt and rocky path ahead of me. The forest floor was covered in roots, wildflowers, and fallen leaves that crunch beneath my feet. I take a breath of the fresh air as the fragrance of leaves and grass flow into my lungs.

At length, we reach the hill path; the stone path rises in rugged perfection. It scrambles steeply upwards. The mountain rose on the horizon. Prodding slowly one behind the other, I begin to use my hands where the path rises steeply with uneven, rocky steps. With each stretch, I reach higher; with each stride, I'm stronger.

'Are we there yet?' asks Luke, puffing.

'No,' Jake responds.

'Are we there yet?' he asks again, panting.

Theo turns and gives him the look as if saying, 'Shut up!'

At last, the day is growing old; the sun sinks downwards to the west. We reach a clearing with a valley opening below.

'We made it!' Luke says as he dramatically collapses to the forest floor.

To my left of the clearing ran a river. Looking through the water of the river was like peering through perfect glass, unsmudged by fingerprints. The small pebbles at the bottom of the river were different shades of brown, grey, and silver.

My reflection staring back at me, my face bright pink from the hike.

'Don't look too long at your reflection. Otherwise, you'll fall in love with it, just like Narcissus,' Theo jokes as he pushes me into the river.

The water cool against my body, my face soaked, the droplets of water running into my eyes and drip from my chin.

Standing, the water comes to my waist. I cup some water into my hands taking a drink; drinking fresh cold water is like the greatest luxury on earth.

'Here,' Theo offers his extended hand as assistance to exit the river.

With a mischievous grin, I accept his hand, pulling him in. Theo lets out a yelp as he falls into the cold water.

Emerging, he wipes the water from his face, moving his hair into place.

'Karma,' I reply.

The breeze of the evening air cool against my bare arms as I help myself out of the river. I stand in a puddle, dripping on the forest floor.

'Theo, come assist us with starting the fire,' Alexandros calls us over.

Theo walks towards the logs and sticks gathered by the others; lifting his hands, he generates flames, starting the fire.

Iris and Luke spread out the sleeping bags around the campfire, close enough to feel the heat but not get burnt.

The sun goes down, making the fire become more vivid and bright; the river nearby has the reflection of a distant glow.

The heat from the campfire seemed to be sucked into the frigid air as Jake adds more wood, poking it with long sticks.

The heat grew, warming us up; orange, red, and faint yellow flames celebrate with their wild dance. The fire projects long shadows on the surrounding area; the light of the flames dance against the trees, mesmerising to watch.

I sit as close as I dared to feel the radiating heat, holding out my cold hands for warmth.

'We will have to nurse it throughout the night for it to last,' suggests Iris.

Luke and Jake return shortly after with more fuel for the fire.

Tucked into a sleeping bag, the night pulls on my eyelids.

CHAPTER 27

One-eyed Beast

We spent the night in Shenandoah National Park, sleeping in the open air, the stars up above flooding the sky. We were all so tired that we fell asleep instantly.

The sun hit my eyes and woke me up very early as it peaks over the mountain, flooding the sky with light.

I awoke, folding my sleeping bag, stretching, eager for the day ahead, putting the fire out before we make our way back down the mountain towards the car.

'Stop!' Theo demands as he puts a finger to his mouth, signaling us to be quiet.

Off in the distance, the sound of a rumbling growl shakes the surrounding trees.

'Just our luck,' complains Alexandros.

The horrific sound came from in front of us.

Making our way closer to the sound, we emerge into another clearing; ahead of us stood a one-eyed giant, a cyclops.

The cyclops was so tall that a grown man would not even reach its knees, its skin looked as hard and rough as armour. It wore clothing made from animal skin.

As it sniffs the air, it began to drool. It could smell us.

Cyclops are known to live in caves in very remote areas, and with our luck, we just ran into one.

Its eye lands on us. Letting out a growl, it begins to charge, the ground shaking with each step.

Holding my sword in hand, adrenaline floods my system. It pumps and beats like it's trying to escape. My eyes widen with fear as my body wants to run the opposite direction. But instead, I remain where I am. All I can do is pray to the gods that we will not die within the next thirty seconds.

Before I know it, Theo has already grabbed his bow and arrow and aimed and fired numerous shots at the cyclops's feet, making it tumble over, giving us time to space ourselves before it picks itself up again.

To my right, I notice Jake had hidden in the safety of the trees, hiding from sight.

I shout to Luke to get behind us. Reluctantly, he follows my command.

Alexandros directs his chant to the cyclops. "Κύκλωπας από τον παρακάτω κόσμο, επιστρέψτε για άλλη μια φορά στο μέρος από το οποίο προήλθατε." *Cyclops from the world below, return once more to the place you came from.*

A huge surge of darkness surrounds Alexandros as it turns into a sword. Taking it in hand, assisted by the darkness, he leaps high into the air, thrashing and thrusting the sword at its upper chest, but to his horror, the sword does minimal damage to its armour-like skin, thus irritating the beast even more.

The cyclops swings its arm at Alexandros, but just before impact, an extremely loud-pitched whistle escapes Theo's mouth. The cyclops bellows out in pain, covering its bloody ears.

My adrenaline surges so fast, I almost vomit; beads of sweat trickling down my brow. I close my eyes, and that's when I begin to feel it, electrical surges coming from within. It feels like I'm about to explode with tremendous electricity from my hands. However, all that comes out is a few sparks that catches alight the cyclops's clothing.

'Sh*t, are you serious? Was that it?' I scream out in frustration.

'Damn . . .,' Theo says unimpressed.

The cyclops, seemingly grinning, rages towards me, swinging its large arm, knocking me to the side. I hit the ground with a thud, pain flaming through my body, leaving me unable to move.

My vision becomes a blur just as I see Tia kneel to the ground, placing both her palms on the forest floor as the ground below begins to shake, making the others tumble over. Alexandros stands opposite her, the cyclops in between them; he stomps his foot on the earth, mimicking her position. They work together.

The ground below the cyclops opens, swallowing the monster, closing again once the cyclops was no longer in sight.

Gathering our breaths, we regain ourselves. The birds begin to chime as if nothing had happened.

Jake rushes towards me, helping me stand up.

My head stings with pain. I can feel blood running down the side of my face.

'You don't look too good,' he says as he studies the wound.

'I don't feel it either.'

Alexandros rushes to my side. 'Girl, you know how to fall,' he says sarcastically.

'It looks worse than it feels,' I reassure him.

'Here, let me have a look at it,' Theo says, pushing Jake aside.

He places his hand over the wound. I feel heat, a sort of warmth. It radiates around the wound, and just like that, the pain was gone, and the wound vanished.

'There we go, all better. Dr. Theo to the rescue. Luckily, the wound wasn't too bad as I can only heal minor injuries.'

Sometime later, after defeating the cyclops, we venture back down the mountain and into the car, heading off to our next destination.

The BMW cruises down the freeway, travelling to South Carolina. I sit in the front passenger seat with so much soft leather around me that I could barely hear the engine roaring. I fiddle with the radio to fill our ears with the latest popular music.

Closing my eyes, I can feel the gentle rise and fall of the road beneath us. I cannot imagine what's in store ahead of us as we've already faced off a Minotaur and a cyclops. What's next?

This whole prophecy ordeal, scary as it is, has given me purpose.

Not long after, we arrive at South Carolina. Looking at the map in my hands, it won't be too long before we reach Charleston.

After dropping the car off, we head directly to the Isle of Palms.

'Did you know the neighboring island is called Sullivan's Island, a site of important battles during the American Revolution and Civil War?' Alexandros says proudly.

'We've got ourselves a historian,' Theo bickers.

'The underworld can be boring at times,' he defends himself.

The beach stretches out alongside the water, the golden sand with just the right amount of warmth; sunshine fills the sky. The smell of the salty sea rushes through my nose as I breathe in the fresh air.

'Right there,' Luke points out. Ahead lay a boat dock with a rustic, white-painted shed.

'We can see if someone can assist us there,' Jake adds.

Walking towards the beach shack, the writing on the wall becomes clearer. Written in peeling blue paint are the words 'Scuba Shack.'

A middle-aged man slouched in a bulky wooden chair. He wore loose linen trousers and a polo shirt, close-cropped dark black hair on top of his head, tanned skin, that made me feel almost pale beside him. Mesmerised by the ocean, he gazes off into the distance. Noticing us, he lifts his head.

'G'day, kids.' When he spoke, it was with an Australian accent. His face was one of confidence. Whatever game this man played; he was not used to losing. He smiles like a long-lost cousin, shaking the boys' outstretched hands, including mine and Tia's, but he also gave her an awkward smile.

'Woof! Woof!'

To the man's left, a chocolate-colored dog runs towards us. It was small enough to fit in a child's arms, its eyes wide as it tilts its head one way and the other. At first, it was curious, barking at us.

But as I lean down with my outstretched hand, it sniffs a few times before taking off towards Tia and licking her hand.

'Aww, thank you.' Tia smiles, patting the dog.

'Meet Bear,' the man says, motioning towards the dog.

'Sir—'

'I'll stop you there. My name is Jiorge, so cut the "sir" cr*p,' Jiorge interrupts Jake.

'Sorry, Jiorge. Is there a way we can hire a boat and scuba gear?'

'Yes, mate, for what purpose?'

'My friends and I would like to go fishing.'

'Fishing with scuba gear?' Jiorge asks confused.

'We like to swim with the fishes,' Tia chimes in.

As if contemplating, Jiorge stares off into the ocean. 'Okay,' he decides. 'You've come to the right place. I'm sure we can strike a deal.'

'Thank you, sir—I mean, Jiorge,' Jake says.

'Damage my boat and you'll be paying for it,' he threatens before leading us towards a small white diving boat. 'My scuba gear is one of the best. Even Poseidon himself envies them,' he boasts, giving us all matching black diving suits.

Tia gives him a look before retrieving her suit.

We change into our scuba gear and board the boat.

CHAPTER 28

Alexandros's POV

T he internal combustion engine roars to life, with our diving gears, masks, snorkels, gloves, fins, scuba tanks, and our very own dive computer to assist us on our search for the *Argo*.

The air, humid but normal as it's a subtropical climate. I throw the anchor overboard in the seabed to hold our position near Folly Beach, applying tension to the rod so that the anchor penetrates the bottom.

'All right, ready?' Theo asks, putting his mask on.

'Yeah, let's find it!' Tia beams, excited for the mission ahead.

'Luke and I will stay on the boat,' suggests Jake.

'Good idea,' I respond. He raises an eyebrow at my remark. 'I'm sorry, man, but after your absence with the cyclops, you're better off observing,' I answer.

Rolling his eyes, he turns his attention to the others.

'We're in the ocean, so we're hopefully safe from the alligators that roam the swamps and coves, but just watch out for the sharks,' says Theo.

'Great. What's worse, alligators or sharks?' asks Iris.

'None, you have me. No need to fear the creatures of the ocean. Daughter of Poseidon right here,' chimes Tia as she sits on the edge of the boat, her back against the water.

'Your tank, mask!' Iris lets out.

Holding her head back, she gently falls backwards. She pops right back up, signaling the okay signal. 'I don't need a mask or tank. I can breathe and see underwater.'

'Oh,' she replies.

With an oxygen tank strapped to my back and two respirators, one to breathe through and the other a spare, I step on to the platform, putting the regulator in my mouth before jumping, followed by Theo and Iris, disappearing immediately into the depths of the ocean.

I can move in any direction; strange sea flowers decorate the sand floor. The coral is alive with seahorses as they sway in the current. The water is uncommonly clear as I can see the depth of the ocean floor. A school of brightly colored fish swim by; it's like being in a different world.

I push slowly through the water with my flippered feet as Tia whizzes past me with no effort at all.

Turning, I see a sea turtle swim towards Tia. She smiles, reaching out towards it, her face drops as soon as she notices it's caught in netting. He's come to her for help. She cuts through the tough netting with a sharp knife, freeing the turtle.

Time passed, and we swam around the depths of Folly Beach with no luck. We head back to the surface to regroup.

'Not down here,' Tia informs Jake and Luke.

'While you were down there, we were monitoring the dive computer to see if there are any deeper locations around here, and on the edge of the map, we think we found one nearby,' Luke says.

'Let's give it a shot,' I say, lifting myself back onto the boat. The next thing I know, I've been thrown to the other side of the deck.

'What was that?!' gasps Luke as he holds on to the metal railings.
'I don't know,' I let out, standing back up.
'No way!' Theo exclaims as he looks over the side of the boat.
'It's a hippocampus!' shouts Iris.

The sea creature was a shade of green. It had the head and front legs of a horse and a horizontal fin tail of a fish, its mane was made up of flexible fins, and its hooves replaced by small-webbed fins. The chariot of Poseidon was drawn by a hippocampus, and they were often the mounts of sea nymphs, mermen, sea elves, and mermaids.

The hippocampus leaps through the air, its body arcs and tail flips and down it goes with a splash, retreating into the ocean.

Tia leans over the boat, her hand wading in the water as the hippocampus swam towards her and licks her hand. She begins to talk to it; the creature starts to nod as if it understood every word that came out of her mouth.

'You wouldn't believe it, but it's Bear,' she says, turning back to us.

'Bear? Wait, you mean the dog?' Jake asks confused.

As if confirming Jake's question, the hippocampus neighs.

'But how?' I ask.

'Shapeshifter—he's a shapeshifter, giving him the ability to turn into a form of animal that the locals wouldn't bat an eye towards,' answers Tia.

'But if Bear is a shapeshifting hippocampus, what about its owner, Jiorge?' questions Theo.

'He knew who we were the moment we stepped foot on that dock,' she responds.

I let out a chuckle. 'How did we not know?' The others look at me confused. 'Come on, guys! A man that owns a pet dog that can transform into a hippocampus, doesn't that seem a bit *fishy* to you?' Tia giggles as she looks around at the others, waiting for them to put the pieces together. 'Jiorge is Poseidon!' I let out.

'Not sure why I didn't notice when we first met him. He did give me a warm look. It all makes sense now,' Tia chimes in.

'You gotta be kidding me. I was in the presence of Poseidon himself,' whines Jake.

'I guess he's keeping an eye on us, especially you, Tia,' questions Iris.

'Yes, he is. That's why Bear's following us,' Tia responds. 'Great news—Bear knows where the *Argo* is. It's right where you thought boys,' she says to Luke and Jake.

'Your mental telepathy is making me question reality,' responds Jake as he takes a seat in one of the vacant boat chairs.

'What are we waiting for? Let's get going,' Iris says as she turns on the boat's engine.

We follow Bear as he leads us further out to sea, the sun still shining brightly in the sky, but it is getting late.

We return into the water, far beneath the surface of the sea. I follow Tia and Bear, kicking deeper into the unknown. I could feel the pressure of the water against my suit. Above me, the glow of the surface becomes more distant and dimmer.

As we go deeper, I can feel the temperature of the water drop dramatically. Below us is an opening, possibly a cave. The bottom floor is festooned with sea vegetation—seaweed, coral, and kelp.

From time to time, I am surprised by a lone fish, invisible until it enters my eyesight.

I glance upward to the surface, and my heart begins to race; I have never been this deep before. My desire to find the *Argo* has gone, and now all I desire is fresh air and a hard surface to put my feet on. I cannot stay down here.

My vision begins to blur. Before I can stop myself, I'm kicking upwards. My head begins to pound. The panic starts like a tightening in my chest, as if my muscles are refusing to let another breath in. My breathing becomes shallow, my thoughts running all over the place. I slowly begin to fade in and out of consciousness.

CHAPTER 29

Anastasia's POV

I wasn't the one who noticed Alexandros black out but Bear himself. I turn to find that he had stopped swimming, like he had given up.

I swim towards him, grasping him in my arms, and head towards the surface. The rest of the party follows closely behind.

No, this cannot be the prophecy the sibyl gave me. I cannot be the cause of Alexandros's death.

The others help lift Alexandros back onto the boat.

I try to stay calm as my eyes met Alexandros's slump form; he wasn't moving.

'What happened?' shouts Iris. There was something in that shout, a deep pain behind it.

'I don't know . . .,' I answer as Iris removes his scuba tank and mask. 'He fainted,' I say as I make Alexandros lay down so more blood can flow to his brain. Hopefully, that can help him gain consciousness.

'Will he be okay?' asks Iris, panic evident in her voice.

My hands trembling as I reach for him, I place my two fingers on his neck and hope to feel a pulse.

Nothing.

I check again—definitely nothing.

'Who knows CPR?' I yell.

'I know!' shrieks Iris as she leans down beside him.

'Call the ambulance!' Jake suggests as Theo slaps him across the back of his head, reminding him we're in the middle of the ocean.

Iris places the heel of her hand on the breastbone of Alexandros' chest, then places her other hand on top of her firsthand and interlocks her fingers. She presses straight down onto his chest at a steady rate of compressions. Then she tilts his head gently and lift his chin up with two fingers, pinching his nose. Placing her mouth over his and blowing steadily and firmly into his mouth for about one second, checking that his chest is rising, before repeating.

His eyes snap open. Water bursts out of his mouth, taking a long deep breath. He tries to sit up.

'He's alive!' I let out. Relief flushes over me—this was not the prophecy of the sybil.

'What happened?' he complains, rubbing his head with his hand.

'You almost drowned!' cries Luke.

I grab a water bottle, giving it to him. 'I think it's best if you sit this dive out.'

He doesn't argue with me but nods in agreement, then turns to Iris with a smile and thanks her. She blushes with acknowledgement.

After checking Alexandros is okay, my eyes fall to the surface of the ocean. I want to go back in there. I need to find the *Argo*.

I dive into the water, escaping what just almost happened on the boat. I won't worry about who I am or who I'll become. In the water, I embrace Bear, and I continue the search for the boat.

I head towards the cave we almost reached. With the increasing pressure, I begin to feel like the water is thickening, like it had suddenly turned to soup.

'Let's try down here,' Bear communicates through our minds as I follow him through a cenote.

After what seems like ages of searching, I feel like all hope is lost. Maybe the *Argo* isn't out here. We've come all this way for nothing.

As I float, that's when a glimmer of light appears above me, a glimpse of hope.

A Nereid, a female spirit of the sea, swims by; her skin pink, her pearl white tail shimmers as she swims towards me.

She smiles at me, a sweet smile, as she leads Bear and I to another cenote. She stops in her tracks, turning to face me.

Grabbing my hand, she places it on the wall of the sea cave, slimy as it feels like moss.

Bright light emerging from my hand, I turn my face, shielding my eyes. Once the light fades, I return my attention to the now-hollow entrance through the cave wall.

Leading me through the entrance, still holding onto my hand, we swim, gliding through the water. The hollow entrance opens up as we burst through the water into an underwater cavern.

The room lights up from all the brightly-lit fishes as they swim around, as if fear meant nothing to them.

We burst through the surface of the water, and to my amazement, I see the *Argo* floating nearby. The boat was straight out of a book— it sat so still, its paint was flaked, showing the colors underneath. Its wood was dark, varnished to a deep mahogany. I could tell this boat had many adventures and travelled countless seas and survived many storms. It lay here, waiting for its next crew since its last voyage with Jason and the Argonauts.

As if by divine command, the boat shines, glistening in the ocean.

We found it! But how will we get it out of here and resurface it high above us on the ocean?

As if reading my mind, the Nereid answers by pointing to my heart, as if signaling, 'You're the daughter of Poseidon. You can do anything.'

I turn around, taking in my surroundings, as I try to figure out a way to resurface the *Argo*.

What would my father do?

Bear swims towards me, holding something in his mouth— my father's trident. I gasp.

Retrieving the trident, grasping it in my hand, I close my eyes, as I think of the *Argo* floating high above on the ocean's surface. I feel a surge of power coming from the trident and then flowing through me.

CHAPTER 30

The Argo

'Look over there!' Luke shouts as he points off into the distance. My eyes follow where he points to see the water begin to bubble, bubbling with such intensity that the water begins to foam up all around it.

A sail splits through the ocean's surface. Not long after, the whole boat emerges from the water.

The boat blossoms right there in the middle of the ocean, with sails that stand proud, billowing in the summer wind. The rest of the boat was made up of solid oak, dark just like any oak on land. Its oars meet the ocean with a form of dignity as it creates waves of its own.

'That's the Argo' Jake exclaims. 'The boat that Jason and the Argonauts sailed from Lolcos to Colchis to retrieve the Golden Fleece.'

As no blueprint survived, no one knows what the ship actually looked like, but we were confident that this was it—the legendary *Argo*. What other boat would have made such a grand entrance?

The boat was magnificent. But the ocean treated the *Argo* like it was a foreign object, thrusting it this way and that, as if the ocean suddenly remembers its voyage with Jason and the Argonauts, like its presence brought forth hidden memories that were locked away.

From beside us, Tia and Bear return to the surface.

'You did it!' says Theo in excitement, helping her back onto the diving boat.

'We have to control the environment so I can start the repairs and improvements. I cannot have the boat rocking this way and that when I'm hammering or changing parts,' informs Jake in a way that was more of a demand than a suggestion.

'I can solve that,' Tia says in high spirits, still on cloud nine after successfully finding the *Argo*.

With the success of her demigod supernatural abilities, she stands on the diving boat, facing out towards the *Argo*. Closing her eyes, she raises her hands.

Sand appears, creating our very own island. It surrounds the *Argo*, raising it out of the water and into a motionless position. The angry waves that surrounded the boat previously have now calmed down. The sand is as golden as the setting sun, looking soft by sight, but by touch, hard enough to walk on without sinking.

'This will work!' marvels Jake, watching in awe like the rest of us.

'I'm definitely not envious yet,' mumbles Theo. 'Daughter of Poseidon really has its perks.'

All that was left was a crew to begin the repairs and improvements of the *Argo*. As if reading my thoughts, Alexandros boasts, 'I guess it's time for my surprise.'

I turn to look at him, confusion evident on my face, unsure what he meant.

With that, he moves to the front of the boat, turning the engine on, driving the boat closer to the sand island.

Stopping the boat, he jumps onto the sand, his eyes going dark as he tilts his head back, arms out as he begins to chant, his voice dark and emotionless.

"Ανακινήστε τη γη, συνδυάστε σαν σκόνη, μετατρέψτε το χώμα σε οστά, οστά σε δέρμα. Αναπνεύστε πάλι, προσφερετέ μου." *Rattle the earth, combine like dust, turn soil to bones, bones to skin. Breathe life once more, offer yourselves to me.*

The evening sun disappears. Dark thundering clouds replace the sky above, darkness surrounding us, frightening away any sense of warmth. The wind howling from every direction makes us shudder on the spot. The temperature dramatically drops, colder than the bottom of the ocean.

To the locals, it must look like a storm was brewing.

That's when the first hand appears, digging its way from beneath the surface of the sand. Alexandros continues chanting as more bony hands appear.

I hear the bones crack as they form together. I recoil in horror as I witness what's occurring in front of me. Their flesh starts to form around the bones, some with their flesh rotting more than others, obviously depending on how long they have been decomposing for. YUCK!

Their hearts black and unbeating, they begin to grope and moan, their jaws dislocating as they do so.

A whole army of the undead appears in front of us, the sea of death.

As they slowly form, their eyes are empty; staring straight at us, their mouths drooling; flesh hanging onto their bones. Some of them look like burn victims; others are just bones.

The whole thing was horrific. They groan inhuman groans. Some look demented, deranged; the stink of rotting corpses fills the air.

Some of the undead didn't look as bad, but they were still horrific, only because they still look human, apart from the torn flesh and the emptiness in their eyes. As they were forming, their bodies begin to be covered with worn armour and weapons. Once they were fully formed, Alexandros stops chanting as the undead army stands there, slouching, waiting for their master's command.

Alexandros straightens his composure, letting out a sigh of accomplishment. Running his hands through his hair, he looks at the undead army in front of him before turning and making eye contact with me.

Crossing his arms over his chest, he says proudly, 'Not what you expected?'

Horrified, confused, concerned, I don't know what I was feeling.

One of the undead lets out a piercing screech and charges towards me with blind fury. I stand there frozen, in shock. Alexandros does nothing, but just before it reaches the boat, it stops, staring right into my soul; its dislocated jaw turns into a lopsided grin.

'Got you!' it snaps.

I stare at the inhuman creature in front of me. I was unable to form any words in my mouth.

Alexandros just laughs at the scene in front of him, my horror being an amusement to him.

'Because that's normal,' Theo states as he recovers from the shock.

"We're working with them...?' Luke says, unsure about the whole situation.

'Wait, is no one going to acknowledge that the thing just spoke?' Jake says, backing towards the other end of the diving boat, as far as he could be from Alexandros and his army.

'The thing has a name,' replies the undead man. 'It's Orion.'

'This is your new crew and team,' Alexandros says. 'All aboard!' he yells as the army of the undead turn and march towards the *Argo*.

CHAPTER 31

Alexandros's POV

I sit there watching Jake and the undead army working on the *Argo* as the wind rustles through my hair.

The heat is unbearable. Jake refuses our assistance, apparently we were making things worse.

My light skin, harsh against my eyes, as the sun reflects off it.

My eyes set on the horizon, arms resting on the diving boat's cold rails.

Waiting. Waiting. Sounds easy, right? With a full bladder, thirsty, hungry, hot, bored, and frustrated.

The whole incident around the blackout and the idea that I almost died still taunts me even though it happened a few days ago. I feel as if I've found my weakness—the depth of the ocean—scared the son of Hades. I don't know about you, but that's definitely something I don't want to be known by. I want to be feared and hated so that I could live my demigod life alone and respected.

From the corner of my eyes, I notice Iris practicing her lightning abilities. She stares at her fingertips, as she starts to harness her powers.

The construction was surreal as the undead move and work as one, helping as they assist Jake. This may be strange for the others, but this is what I've been brought up with and known all my life.

Tia and Luke duel with each other, practicing and becoming more skillful with every round. Theo, off in the distance, was shooting at handmade targets.

I want the air conditioning of the mall, not this sun-burning land of sand. In this heat, I can barely form a thought. No cooling breeze to shield us from the sun, I grab the thin fabric of my shirt, waving it in and out, creating a bit of air flow.

'We need more supplies!' Jake shouts towards us from behind one of the masts.

'What more could you possibly want?' Theo complains as we had constantly gone to town gathering supplies.

'You want this job done?'

Theo huffs in defeat, 'Fine.'

'I'll need tantalum and a stock-up of food,' he replies.

'What do the undead eat?' Luke asks.

'Human flesh,' I say jokingly. With no amusement from the others, I add, 'They have no need to eat. They're dead.'

A flush of relief spreads across Luke's face.

'Tan—what?' asks Tia.

'Tantalum—it's one of the strongest metals in the world, but I need it because it's corrosion-resistant.'

'And where will we find this metal?' I ask.

'I know they have stored tons of tantalum in a building in Charleston. It was only just delivered from the Congo. Just waltz right in and ask them for it. Not that hard,' Jake says, returning to work.

'I'll go,' I volunteer.

Iris, Tia, and Luke slowly walk away, not wishing to go into town on a hunt for this metal.

'Ugh . . . fine,' mumbles Theo. 'Let's go.'

Theo and I make our way inland with Jake's directions in hand. Taking the diving boat with us, once we reached the shore, we head straight towards our destination.

'Alexandros.'

'Yeah?'

'I don't like Jake, nor do I trust him,' Theo says.

'You're not the only one that thinks that.'

'Did you see the man in the blue sports hoodie at the marketplace?' he asks.

'You saw him too?'

'Yeah, and something was off.'

'Just keep your eyes and ears open. You and the girls are the only people I trust right now,' I say. The lies I fear the most are the ones that are close enough to be the truth as they run right past you undetected.

'What? Did I hear that correctly? Did Alexandros just admit to trusting people?' Theo jokes.

I ignore him as we continue to walk down the streets of Charleston.

The crowd has a life of its own; their bright clothes shine under the light of the sun. It's busy for sure, but the hustle and hum of chatter brings the city to life.

The tantalum metal was named after Tantalus, an evil man from Ancient Greece. *(Yes, the Greeks play a huge part in influencing the world.)* The metal is rare, very hard, and blue grey in color. Its melting point is 3,020°C, but that will be no problem for Jake.

'There,' Theo points out towards an old building with a large sign above the doors that states, 'Science Labs.' It towers over the other buildings that surround it, blocking the sunlight. It was made of plain bricks, smoked glass, and steel, with multiple windows, and two double doors at the front completing the look.

'Let's get this over with,' I mumble as we head straight towards the entrance.

Opening the double doors, the bell rings above us, informing the receptionist that someone had entered the facility.

An old lady hides from behind the marble counter, her Asian features visible as soon as she pops her head up to greet us.

'Morning. How can I help you today?'

Theo improvises, taking the character of a young apprentice scientist. 'Ma'am, we are here as assistant trainers. It's our first day. Would you be kind enough to point in the direction of your labs and metal storage facilities?'

'Oh right, just need you to sign in,' she says as she hands us a clipboard and pen. I cannot believe that she didn't even ask for ID, must be her first day also.

After signing our names as 'Jake Pearson' and 'Seth Jacobs,' she gives us directions towards Lab 142.

The hallways were made up of white metallic roof and white metallic floors. Every footstep echo around us, not loudly but enough to let others know we were approaching.

After a few minutes, we were standing outside Lab 142. I slowly turn the door handle.

Inside the lab, it was dimly lit through the partially-open blinds, nothing but machinery inside. The lab was quiet and cold. Turning on the main lights, the room—clean, organised, efficient—becomes more visible. White coats hang against one side of the wall. Across the back wall, floor-to-ceiling windows reveal a view of the surrounding city buildings.

'Let's have a look in here,' Theo suggests as he walks towards a huge walk-in refrigerator. Inside lay test tubes and small containers of various kinds of substances and metals.

'Found the tantalum,' Theo says as he shows off a small container towards the back of the cabinet.

'I think we're going to need a lot more than that,' I add, looking at the small container in his hands, definitely not big enough for Luke's magic.

'Where are we going to find a large amount of this metal?'

'Hopefully, there should be a storage area in the sub levels of the building. That's where they keep their huge supplies of whatever they need,' I say, looking around the lab one last time.

Leaving the science lab behind, we head off again to the lower levels of the building in hopes we will find the large storage containers holding the tantalum.

We stumble upon the basement level with no access card needed. We carefully walk through the door.

Unlike the lab room, the basement level was lit up before entry, dark blue metallic walls and floors all around us. Aisles of large containers as far as the eye could see littered the floor and a couple of forklifts and small delivery trucks.

'We're going to have to find the needle in the haystack,' I say with dread, looking at all the aisles we will need to look through.

'I'll start from this end, and you start on the other side. Shout out if you find them,' I say as I walk towards the far left, going through all the aisles in search for any containers labelled tantalum.

Upon what feels like hours of searching, I hear Theo shout, 'Bingo!'

I stop my search within the aisle and hurry towards him. 'You found it?!' I say with relief.

Looking at the containers in front of us, the words 'Tantalum' were written all over them.

'Yeah, but we will need to use the forklift to move them and borrow one of those delivery trucks for transport back to the diving boat.'

'Acting like a thief?' I ask.

'How else do you manage to transport them?' Theo argues.

'You know what, let's leave morals behind and get this job done,' I agree.

I make my way towards one of the trucks. Finding the keys in the ignition, everything is falling into place quite easily. I was expecting it to be a lot harder. I turn the engine on, and it hums to life. Theo uses the forklift to load up the containers.

We leave the basement level through the roller doors and out onto the open streets. The whole event, to our surprise, was remarkably easy, as there were no obstruction from any security, as if we were assisted by the gods.

After stopping to refill our food supply, we drive back towards our docked diving boat, loaded the tantalum containers, and ditched the 'borrowed' truck.

In the twilight, the beach was the color of tinted brown, the sand orange and soft on the eyes, the water dark as we headed towards the *Argo.* Tomorrow we set sail.

CHAPTER 32

Anastasia's POV

Today we set sail.

A strong wind was blowing. With the breaking waves, the sea became white. Just the right weather for the start of our journey.

Nervous about the voyage ahead, I was not alone; everyone else was anxious also, everyone but Jake. He looks unfazed, making it more concerning, as if he were aware of the outcome.

The *Argo* was fashioned with ancient oak, dark rich timbers, browns close enough to be black. The large masts that stand tall, instead of its old sails, were now adorned by sails of white. The newly improved *Argo* brought forth an eagerness for a new great adventure.

It was a confident form of faith, the feeling in our bones that we could achieve anything. We began this quest feeling uncertain about finding the lost legendary ship. But now that we have found it, we believe we can do anything.

It's quite amazing how Jake did all this in a matter of days; the metal retrieved by Theo and Alexandros was used to smear the outside of the boat, making it stronger against the pounding waves.

I place my hand into the water, feeling the strength of Poseidon's domain under my fingertips as the water moves softly around my hand. Pulling my fingers out and watching the droplets of water drip, they fall as if snatched by gravity, retreating into the ocean below. I could stay here all day.

I do find it strange that we are aboard the legendary *Argo* and the crew consists of the undead. But seeing and being a part of unusual things is kind of normal for demigods; even so, it's hard to get used to.

As the winds become stronger, we open the sails as they inhale the air, bright in the sunshine.

Iris held tight on to the railings of the boat, her knuckles white as she held on. She leans forward, feeling the salt spray of the ocean. I stand beside her. I squint as I look at the sight of the waves. A layer of salt soon forms on my face. Licking my dry lips, I taste the salty ocean.

The Bermuda Triangle is located north of the Atlantic Ocean. It has been told that things suddenly disappear, by supernatural forces, as they enter this relatively unknown area. Over the centuries, many ships and planes have gone missing, never to be found again.

Many believe that the lost islands of the Kingdom of Atlantica were part of the many things that disappeared within the Bermuda Triangle. The founders of Atlantica were half-gods, half-humans *(demigods)*. The Kingdom was made up of concentric islands that were separated by wide moats, linked by a canal that ran through the centre. The island contained gold, silver, and many other precious metals, rare exotic wildlife, and lush fields. The capital city of the Kingdom of Atlantica was named Atlantis, which sat dead centre of the islands.

The Greek gods became angry with the demigods on Atlantica as they had lost their way; the people became greedy, petty, and irrational. As punishment, the gods sent one terrible night of fire and earthquakes that caused Atlantica to sink into the ocean.

The Ancient Greek philosopher Plato wrote about the destruction of the Kingdom of Atlantica as he tried to warn the mortals of what may happen to them if they disobey or anger the Greek gods.

In front of me the flat sea stretched in all directions, the afternoon sun scattering sparkles across the surface of the ocean, a line of dark blue curves the horizon.

★☆★

We have been aboard the *Argo* for two days now as we near the Bermuda Triangle.

Alexandros's dead army move around the boat. As they sail us forward, I begin to feel less connected to the water as we leave Poseidon's domain into the realm of forbidden voyage. *Note that Poseidon does not have domain over cursed waters.*

'The compass, it's stopped working!' Jake cries as he shows us.

'We're getting closer. The compass is showing erratic readings. The magnetic force is deflecting the needle and making it spin in all directions,' I say, taking a closer look at the compass.

That's when we feel it—salt-kissed air whips around us, whispering warnings.

'Return.'

'If you go further, Poseidon will ignore your cries.'

'There is no hope beyond this point.'

Looking over the side of the boat, we see the sea nymphs pleading for us to turn back.

I turn away, making eye contact with Theo, his face expressionless as he listens to the warnings of the sea nymphs.

'All hands-on deck!' yells Alexandros. I whip my head to the direction we're heading.

We have heard stories of the monstrous waves of the Bermuda Triangle that appear out of nowhere, crushing anything in its way, smashing even the sturdiest boat, ripping it into splinters and leaving nothing. But nothing could have prepared us, for what was about to take place.

Black clouds swirl above us; blue-grey waves begin to form below us, crashing against the side of the *Argo*, pulling us into the unknown.

The wind tears harshly against the sails. The undead assist in bringing the sails down, otherwise, they will be ripped apart by the howling wind of the upcoming storm.

'Life jackets on—now!' Theo barks.

Everyone retrieves their life jackets, putting them on for safety reasons. We don't need anyone drowning before we've even reached our destination.

Just as we thought the storm ahead couldn't get any worse, the thunder rumbles through the clouds, bringing forth thick, dark, blinding rain.

The rain was heavy, we couldn't see the person beside us; only the neon yellow of their life jackets was visible.

'Hold on!' I can barely hear Iris yell.

But it was too late—a monstrous wave knocks Theo and I overboard, along with most of the undead. With no control over the forbidden water, I thrash about as the dark indigo water closes around me, filling me with dread. Breaking through the surface, I try to locate Theo.

'I'm okay!' he emerges from the water, trying to catch his breath.

Wave after wave crashes against the *Argo*, tumbling us deeper into the unknown water. I don't worry about myself as I can breathe underwater, but Theo is down here with no scuba tank.

As I pop back up to the surface, I notice Theo does the same with the assistance of his life jacket, only to be pulled back under with another wave that hits. This time I sink faster; panic has my heart hammering against my ribs.

My legs struggle as they push me towards the surface. All I can hear are the crashing waves and the shouting of the undead sailors; the swirling waves and currents pull us under again.

I need to find Theo.

I break through the surface once again. I'm noticing my abilities are starting to wane. Gulping for air, I look around frantically.

'Theo!' I yell.

The panic of finding Theo consumes me as I forget to close my mouth as I tumble over and cold-water rushes in.

Chocking.

Please don't let this be it. I cannot breathe. My head is pounding. Every cell in my body is screaming for oxygen. I keep fighting for air.

Red and black splotches dance in front of me; the coldness that I felt entering the water has completely disappeared.

'Don't give up!' someone shouts in my mind as a brilliant gold flash to what I think appears to be a *trident*.

My eyes snap back open. No way a few rouge waves are going to prevent me from fulfilling this prophecy. With a surge of strength that suddenly takes over my body, I swim to the surface.

'Tia!' screams Theo.

I see Theo as he struggles to keep himself afloat. I swim towards him, grabbing on to his arm, pulling him to the direction of the shouts that belong to the remaining crew of the *Argo*.

Reaching the edge of the *Argo*, trying to avoid being crushed by the waves against the hull, I yell out towards the others, hoping my cries are loud enough to be carried over the storm.

I see a rope ladder being thrown overboard. 'Climb!' shouts Luke, his curly hair now stuck to his face from the rain. With a mighty lunge, I time my grasp of the ladder as it almost swings past me.

I help Theo climb up the ladder as he slowly makes his way back onto the *Argo*. I follow closely behind. I use all my strength, pulling myself up. Holding on for dear life, I brace against the impact of every wave. The cold storm air against my back makes the climb harder as I shiver upon every move.

Luke helps me up over the railing, just in time before another wave hits, knocking us onto the floor of the boat, washing us to the other side. We barely grab the rails before falling off the edge.

'You've got to be kidding me!' Alexandros yells.

Another monstrous wave knocks us all over the *Argo*. I gather my strength, standing back up, the cold storm air harsh against my bare arms.

The wheel of the boat was spinning frantically around. I rush towards it, holding it onto its course, straight ahead.

The *Argo* rushes forward, piercing through each wave.

CHAPTER 33

My Evil Foe Zorander

The sun replaces the storm clouds as we emerge through the barrier into the Bermuda Triangle.

The sea disappears from view, replaced by a seemingly screen of vegetation, the atmosphere damp.

The island looks as beautiful as every Caribbean island, the colors almost too intense to be realistic. Shimmering blue waters, sparkle in the presence of the sunlight, encircle the island. Greenery spreads out, green pine trees, rainforest, sandy white beaches, I could go on and on.

In the distance, a volcano waiting to erupt, it seems like it's been simmering for ages; the white wisps rise from the top. The sides of the volcano are much like any other regular mountain covered with dead and living trees.

The darkness and pure evil hid within the island. If you looked at it, you would not expect it, but the closer you got, the more on edge you felt as you start to see all the flaws.

'We made it!' Theo says excitingly.

Everyone, still drenched from the storm, looking a lot like drowned rats.

'Drop the anchor, Alexandros commands the few remaining undead.

'You expect us to swim?' complains Jake.

'The water is beautiful,' Tia marvels.

Throwing my sword and scabbard overboard, breaking the water's surface, I dive into the water after it.

The water oddly warm against my skin, I emerge to the surface with my sword and scabbard in hand. The ocean is very clear below me, so much so that it was impossible to guess the depth. The coral below could be five feet down or thirty. I can see the school of bright fish and sea flowers and plants that decorate the ocean floor.

'What are you waiting for?' I ask the others as they stare at me from the top of the boat.

Luke jumps in after me. He swims towards me, blowing air bubbles with his knife in hand. 'Come on!' yells Luke as he swims around me childishly.

That's when the realisation hit me—he's just a boy, sixteen. He should be enjoying school, making friends, not having to worry about the darkness that really runs through this world. But instead, he is here with us, completing a dangerous prophecy.

I make a promise to myself. He is my brother. Once this is all over, I will protect him from this harsh world. I'll help him live a safe and protected life.

My concern must be evident on my face as he questions if I'm okay.

'Yeah.' I respond. 'Just thinking.'

He smiles before facing his attention to the others diving into the ocean.

We swim, making our way towards the island.

My sea legs almost give way as I plant my feet onto the sand.

The island seems to be uninhabited; it was silent, too silent.

'Zorander probably knows we're already here,' Luke suggests. 'He has eyes and ears everywhere. We have to be careful. Look out for each other, or we won't be getting off this island alive.'

'Where do we start?' I ask.

'The volcano,' Alexandros suggests, motioning with his head towards the steaming volcano. 'Where else would a villain live?'

Taking a huge breath in, looking around, facing the others, I try to read their facial expressions.

Jake looks forward before heading off towards the volcano, not making eye contact with any of us.

'You okay?' I ask, walking up to him.

'Um . . . yeah. Why wouldn't I be?' he says, brushing me off.

Cutting our way through the dense, thick undergrowth, the air moist and still. Trees tall as they surround us, blocking out any sort of sunlight.

The further we walk towards the centre of the island, the stronger the stench of evil was.

A strange red light shimmers through the canopy of the trees, shining directly above us. Peering up, I look at the light, confused how it suddenly appeared and for what reason.

Up ahead, mist swallows the base of the volcano. It smothers the greenery, underbrush, and tree trunks. The colors of the forest fade away. Now everything was the same grey as the mist.

'This way,' Theo leads as he finds an entrance through the volcanic mountain; we follow him down a dirty path that opens into a hollow entrance.

'Too easy,' I mumble.

Looking around, I look for anything out of place, and that is when I see it—a flaming arrow heading directly for us.

'Move!' I yell at the group, scattering out. The arrow barely misses us.

'We've been waiting for you.'

We turn to see that the voice belongs to a young blonde-haired girl, bow raised in her hand aimed directly at us, ready to fire again.

'Traitor,' recognises the girl as she eyes down Luke. 'Zorander will not be pleased with you.'

Placing my hand on Luke's quivering arm, I address the girl in front of us. 'And you are?'

'Cleo, daughter of Athena.'

'Well, Cleo, daughter of Athena, where can we find this all-powerful being called Zorander?' I ask sarcastically.

Her emotionless face turns into a smirk. 'Right this way.'

'You expect us to just follow you?' Theo questions her. 'It could be a trap,' Theo whispers to me.

'What do you mean could be? It is a trap,' I whisper.

'No. You're right. I'm not asking you. I'm telling you,' she demands.

'Ooh, frightening,' Theo mimics.

'Cut it out, boy,' demands another demigod—red-haired, looking about the same age as us—who suddenly appears from our left.

'There's more of you?' asks Theo.

As if what he said was a key word, more demigods appear, ten to twenty of them, all at once, surrounding us, cutting off any means of escape.

'You and your big mouth,' hisses Tia.

'Are you going to tell them or am I?' asks the red-haired boy.

'What?' I question.

Jake steps out from beside me, standing in line with the lost demigods opposite us.

'Jake?' I ask, this cannot be happening.

'Traitor!' yells Alexandros. 'I knew there was something up with you from day one!' he adds.

Oh, how quickly love can turn into hate without the need of fighting. You just let the negative emotion in as it tugs at your soul. I fought for sympathy to be kind, to hear his side of things, but the very terrible thing I had predicted had come true.

Jake was a traitor, a soul-less backstabbing scoundrel.

'Don't act like you wouldn't do the same if you were given the opportunity,' Jake responds.

'That's how they knew where we were. You were feeding them intel on our whereabouts,' Theo includes.

'You're fools, fighting on the wrong side. The gods don't give a damn about us. We're just pawns in their games,' Jake tries to reason.

'Don't go pulling that string on us, boy. If Luke can see that, what you're doing here is completely wrong. Then how blind are you?' argues Alexandros.

I turn to see that Luke did not like being involved in this argument and stood behind us, wishing to not be included.

Through all this bickering, Tia stands there silently, unsure and awestruck at the situation unfolding in front of her.

'I chose this, and so should you,' Jake persists, as if he truly believed that what they were doing was right.

'I understand that the gods are not the most caring parents, but how can you blame them when they see so many of their children die in front of them? We're not immortals like they are. We can die!' I shout.

Too much hatred becomes a sickness of the mind, heart, and soul. For where hatred has claimed its possession, there is no room for love, sympathy, or forgiveness. If you leave it to just bottle up, hate can completely poison your soul. Jake's need for revenge was evident, and the only way that he could be cured was for him to act on it, the cold art of revenge.

'That's enough!' yells the red-haired boy. 'This bickering is getting boring.'

'Let's not keep him waiting any longer. This way,' Cleo says as she walks us further down a windy path into the volcano.

The path steeps further into the heart of the island. Taking us deeper in, each step we take furthers us from the safety of the surface.

All of us are on edge, as we follow the lost demigods towards their master Zorander.

CHAPTER 34

Zorander's POV

I Don't know why I choose these pathetic demigods to do my job. They're completely hopeless. I should have done this myself.

"Klaus, wrong one!"

It's kind of a downside working with kids—they complain all day.

'Zorander, I'm tired, I can't train anymore.'

'Does it look like I care? Leave me alone. I've got my own problems to deal with. I don't need to hear yours.'

'Sir, the vrykolakas won't drink out of the blood bags I've given them.'

'Complaining about a problem without providing a solution is called whining. Figure it out, Klaus,' I growl at the annoying boy in front of me. 'Let them take a sip from your wrist,' I suggest.

The boy's eyes open in horror. 'Nooo—no, sir.'

'I'm not arguing with you. Give them some blood before they go on a rampage feeding off every one of you!'

The boy quickly scurries away with the full blood bags in hand, giving it another shot.

How do I describe myself? Ancient, historic, antique . . . I'm old, very old.

All these words to describe me. *A Titan.*

My name is Aetius. Ring any bells? No, of course not. I was erased from all the history books, those pathetic gods.

I am the son of Uranus and Gaea, so yes, that does make me a Titan. You must be thinking, 'How is that possible? There are only twelve Titan children,' but no, there are thirteen. But I wasn't a child they dared to boast about, let alone claim as their own.

It all started centuries ago, at the beginning of time. My siblings and I rebelled against our father, who had abandoned us in Tartarus. We decided to follow my youngest brother Cronus, and we defeated our father, Uranus. We made Cronus our new ruler. Zeus, son of Cronus, rebelled against us *(runs in the family)*. I was the only Titan who fought with Zeus and his siblings against my family who sided with Cronus.

Ten years of endless battles and we eventually won the Titanomachia war. My brothers and sisters were imprisoned by Zeus, hurling them down into a cavity beneath Tartarus.

You must be thinking, 'That's not too bad. Why are you starting an uprising over that?' Well, reader, we haven't even gotten to the good part yet.

Zeus doubted my loyalty, so he sent me off on a quest. Little did I know that this quest was a trap. My fate had already been determined.

Zeus gave me control over a rising kingdom, known to you as Germany. I didn't want much in life, believe it or not, but I was pleased to call this kingdom my own.

Everything was perfect. My kingdom was growing. There was no other who could stand against the might of my armies. But fate got the best of me. My second in command, Teressa, who was my most beautiful partner and who I trusted with my life, was always beside me as we ransacked each village across Europe. But unknown to me, until it was too late, Zeus also fancied her.

One fateful evening, Teressa told me that Zeus was trying to bed her, so I went to confront him. When I arrived at Mount Olympus, he was nowhere to be seen. I hurried back to my kingdom to find it burning up in flames. I ran to the royal chamber to find Teressa had been brutally murdered. I turned to find Zeus staring at me. I asked him why. He responded by striking me down with one of his legendary lightning bolts.

Zeus and the rest of the gods thought they had gotten away with murdering me. But they did not know that a Titan could regenerate, if not decomposed properly, in the depths of Tartarus. It had only taken me a thousand years. But now I'm back, and the gods are going to pay.

I've been turning their very own offspring against them right under their noses. Nobody suspected a thing as I gained the trust of these dim-witted demigods. I built a bond so deep that they may as well have been my own.

Just like any hunter, I find their weakness and use it to exploit them. In this situation, it's their lust for their missing parents.

You probably think I'm a psychopath.

Legend says that my heart died long ago with my original body. This is what gives me the ability to kill without guilt. I've been rolling around in my grave for centuries, thinking of a way to make them all suffer, suffer like they did to me.

I have dreamt of revenge ever since, and no one will stop me. Definitely not the four prophesied demigods.

I've taken the name Zorander, making them think I am just one of those lonely demigods. They won't know what hit them until it's too late.

'Sir, they're here.'

I sit up in my cobblestone throne. 'Bring them in.'

A smile makes its way onto my face. *It has begun!*

'Here are the so-called legendary demigods,' I bellow as I look at them. They pan out in front of me, their eyes turn stone cold as soon as they land on me.

'The traitor, what a pleasure to see you again,' I say, narrowing my eyes at Luke. 'You had one job, boy, and you turned against me. You deserve their fate.'

Luke turns away, eyes falling to the floor.

CHAPTER 35

⟨⁂⟩

Vrykolakas and Lycanthropes

The lost demigods lead us into an enormous room, dimly lit torches chasing the shadows away. The walls were made up of stone, rugged-looking, with red banners hanging against the wall, a Labyrinth symbol adorned the centre of the banner.

In the middle of the room sat a lonely throne made of cobblestone, crested with jewels and decorative metals, forming an elegant coat. Light from the ceiling above, lit up the throne and the middle-aged man that sat upon it, Zorander.

The cold look that reflects on his face gave me shudders. His hands were tightly closed around the arm rest of the throne. He seems to have no sense of humanity, his heart had to be formed from stone, an evil glint shone in his dark eyes.

Just before the throne, engraved on the floor, were the symbols of the Olympian gods.

The throne room was cold, sending a shiver down my body as I enter.

'Here are the so-called legendary demigods,' he bellows, retrieving a stone-cold stare. 'The traitor, what a pleasure to see you again,' he says as he narrows his eyes at Luke. 'You had one job, boy, and you turned against me. You deserve their fate.'

'Why are you doing this?' I manage to let out.

He stares at me intently before responding. 'Revenge. I want to finish what my siblings started.'

'Siblings?' asks Tia.

As he replies, his eyes go darker. 'I am the son of Uranus and Gaea.'

'You're a Titan?' Tia lets out.

'No, your anus.' Theo snickers.

'Shut up, fool!' yells Zorander.

The Titans were a powerful race that ruled the world before the Olympians. But the man in front of us looked like a mere mortal, nothing like a giant overpowering Titan.

'Well, that just took an unexpected turn,' Tia whispers, loud enough for me to hear.

'You've come just in time!'

'In time for what?' Alexandros finally speaks up.

Zorander's wicked grin widens. 'For the games.'

We look amongst ourselves, confused. What games?

'Andrew and Sebastian, take our visitors to the dungeon until we are ready for them,' he demands two of the hovering demigods.

They drift down and walk towards us, iron chains in hands. 'Just for precaution,' one of them says as they forcefully apply them, simultaneously removing our weapons.

They lead us away, everyone that is, except Jake, down another hallway deeper into the volcano.

'Welcome to your new accommodation.' One of the boys snickers.

Ahead of us, at the end of the chamber, lay large double doors with stairs leading downwards, the floor uneven, making it harder to move. In the gloom, all I could make out were the iron-barred walls.

'Get in,' says one of the boys, pushing us into the cell.

'Gear up,' the other one says.

'Gear, what?' I ask, turning to see different suits of armour strewn against the back wall—chest plates, lances, cuisses, knee cops, tasses, brassards all the pieces that make up a set of full-body armour.

'I'm not wearing that,' I utter.

'Then you'll die easily in the arena,' responds the other demigod.

'Arena?' asks Tia.

'You'll find out tomorrow,' says the boy, laughing as they walk away.

'Guess we have no choice. If we want to live, we need to suit up. We have no idea what to expect tomorrow,' I give in.

The dungeon cell was a hollow square of concrete, one way in and one way out. Given enough time in here, the isolation would lead a person to forget their name and identity, driving them mad.

Surrounded by walls, there was nothing else to do but stare at them. In silence, we sat; my back against the cold concrete wall, waiting.

'We're up against a Titan,' Tia breaks the silence.

'Did you know about that, boy?!' Theo says, pushing Luke, holding him up by his collar, against the dungeon wall.

'Put him down,' I demand.

'No, no. I had no idea,' Luke manages to let out with a gulp.

A few silent moments pass before Theo lets him down.

'This is great, just great,' Theo declares in defeat, shaking the iron bars that hold us captive.

'You'll be out soon, demigod,' one of the boys snap, spitting at Theo.

'You're going to regret that,' Theo responds through clenched teeth.

'Let it go, Theo,' Tia mumbles, as she pulls him away from the bars.

'What are we going to do?' I ask, not realising that I had just spoken aloud.

'We're the children of the Olympian gods. We can get through this. This isn't over, not by a long shot,' Tia demands.

Eventually, Luke speaks up. 'There's something I have to tell you, and you're not going to like it.'

Theo shoots him a glare.

'The games that Zorander mentioned earlier, they're sort of a sport that he uses to frighten us into order. I've only seen the game take place once during the years I've been here. I think we're going to be the main attraction,' he lets out.

'Go on!' Theo snaps, impatient as always.

'He would send anyone that rebelled against him into the arena, where you'd have to fight against a monster of his choosing.'

'What type of monster?' asks Alexandros, finally contributing to our conversation.

'Vrykolakas and lycanthropes.'

He must have seen the confusion on my face. "Vrykolakas are the undead Ancient Greek ancestors of vampires, except much worse. After draining their victims dry, they would eat their flesh. Lycanthropes are shapeshifters, they can transform into werewolves.'

'Great, just great. Can't wait for tomorrow,' Theo mutters sarcastically.

'Son of Hades, don't these creatures come from the Underworld?' Adds Theo.

'Only the vrykolakas.'

'Then why are they up here?'

'I don't know . . . must have escaped somehow—'

'Are you good for anything?!' Theo snaps, tension building between the two.

'Theo—' I warn.

'No Iris, all he does is sulk around, hating the world above. If it's so bad, why don't you go back to HELL!' he shouts.

'I've had about enough!' Alexandros growls at Theo, before storming off to the other end of the cell, away from the others. I subconsciously stand up and follow after him.

'I'm done with the stereotypes.' he says as soon as he notices me behind him. I stare at him sympathetically, silently ushering him to continue.

'My father is the god of the Underworld, and do you know what I have to do to stay up to those standards... living under his shadow? I know the stories the kids at the Olympic Sanctuary say about me, they aren't very quiet. How I'm just like my father-mean, horrible, uncaring monster.'

He falls against the wall, leaning his head back, 'I'm not evil.'

Turning to face me, his eyes showing that of only kindness.

'Alexandros, you're nothing like your father. Just because your dad may be all that, doesn't mean you are. You're one of the kindest people I know.' I respond, sitting right down beside him.

'Stuff what the others at school think about you. All that matters is your own opinion, and how you think about yourself.' I say, leaning my head on his shoulder, 'I find you quite charming actually.'

He looks down at me, 'Oh I know.' I could hear the smile in his voice.

CHAPTER 36

Last Goodbyes

W e stumble out via an underground passageway, and through a large metal gate into an open arena, the sun blinding as our eyes had been adjusted to the darkness of the dungeons.

I blink a few times, slowly adjusting to the light. Looking around, I see that we are standing at the entrance of what seems to be a stadium, standing on a wooden floor, covered in a layer of sand.

The grand arena was circular. There were large stone slabs, which gave the spectators places to sit. They descend steeply towards the pit, where we stood. The spectator seats where covered, shielded from the glaring rays of the sun, giving them maximum visibility on what was about to take place down below in the pits.

It looks a lot like one of those gladiator pits in Ancient Rome.

The hot blast of the sun pours down on us. I could almost feel Helios in his chariot directly overhead.

I feel like our quest was being watched. The gods of Mount Olympus tracking our every move, placing bets on the odds of our survival.

I scan the auditorium. There would be somewhere close to two thousand spectators. The crowd was hungry with excitement, moving around for the best seats, cheering, and shouting as soon as they notice us.

'Welcome to the games!' a loud voice booms, 'Per tradition, the games will now commence. The prophesied demigods are going to give us a show,' the voice continues with a hint of sarcasm. 'You will die here. Do your best to entertain.'

The main voice belongs to Zorander. I can see him standing in one of the spectator seats, accommodating the crowd.

My senses are assaulted by a blinding light and the roar of thousands of voices.

He rubs his hands together in the way villains do. He was not going to pretend to be anything other than what he was. He enjoyed it, being a monster. Our lives mean nothing as this was all just a game to him.

I recognise my sword and scabbard as one of the boys thrusts them into my hands.

We are forcefully pushed towards the centre of the arena. Once there, the boys remove our metal cuffs and chains. Once they retreat through the metal gate that we emerged from, Zorander speaks again. 'Release the vrykolakas and lycanthropes.' He breaths in deeply. 'And let the *games begin*!'

The deafening sound of metal levers rotating fills the air as the iron gate opposite us begins to crack open, and that is when we hear it— the screeching cries and terrifying howls.

They emerge from the darkness, about twenty to thirty in total. The vrykolakas have skin so pale it resembles the full moon. Their eyes, just like that of a cat, alert but the color of blood. Sharp fangs were protruding over their blood-stained lips; their voices eerie as they speak.

Behind them came the lycanthropes. Their growls made us shudder on the spot. Their fur thick, but their eyes are human. They have the killer instinct of a wolf pack, communicating through barks and grunts as they circle around us, cutting off any means of escape. They were almost indistinguishable from real wolves, except that they were larger and moved with the intelligence of a human.

If this were a different situation, I wouldn't fear them as they protect humans. They do not kill without a purpose. Lycanthropes should not be feared. They are known to protect until their last breath. But not in this situation. Under Zorander's influence and control, they know no better.

Luke lets out a shuddering shriek, looking up at me, inching behind me, trying to hide himself.

'Hey, we got this,' I try to reassure him.

The Lycanthropes' ears perk forward, and their mouths turn into a snarl, revealing their sharp-edged canines.

'Well, it was great knowing you all,' Theo says sarcastically, receiving a deadly glare from Tia.

'Stop, you're frightening the boy,' Alexandros spits.

Our weapons held steady in hand as the monsters glare at us. The crowd cheering, as to them, we are the villains.

The first sign that the monsters where about to attack was the stance that they all took, ready to pounce at any given moment.

As the battle begins, the shouts of the crowd fade into the background, adrenaline filling my veins.

A single vrykolakas grabs my attention as it's the first to lunge towards me. Its spear in hand, it thrusts, but I counter it quickly and brush it aside with my sword. The vrykolakas hisses, showing off its fangs. It pounces towards me in super speed I didn't have time to process. A sudden gush of pain jolts throughout my body as I slam onto the ground. It grabs my throat with its hands tightening around my neck. I try to gasp for air. It bites, digging its fangs into my shoulder. I let out a yelp. I feel it start to drain my blood. I retaliate, grabbing on to its hands that still clench around my neck. I try to concentrate as I feel sparks start to form. I shock it, and it releases its grip on me.

This is my chance. I retrieve my sword from the ground and in one motion, thrust it into its bare stomach. It looks at me unfazed.

'Aim for the heart!' Tia shouts towards me, noticing my predicament.

I remove and thrust again, this time right into its heart. The vrykolakas takes its last breath before crumbling to ash.

Tia channels her power from within, wiping out a whole group of vrykolakas with saltwater. They begin to burn from the salt, disintegrating to ash.

Alexandros uses dark mist to taunt and distract the lycanthropes as Theo shoots flaming arrows at them. Luke thrushes his sword about, decapitating any lycanthropes that comes too close to him, his sword dripping with their blood.

We fight together as we destroy each lycanthrope and vrykolakas that attacks. Soon nothing stood before us.

I regain my breath, my heart still pounding in my chest. Luke smiles at me, whispering, 'You were right, we did it.'

'No!' bellows Zorander from the safety of his seat. 'This was not how it was supposed to unfold.' He stands, staring at us in disgust.

'What? Not expecting the children of the gods to defeat your minions? You've got to do better than that,' provokes Theo.

'Oh, this does not end here,' Zorander responds.

'You seriously have to learn to keep your mouth shut,' Tia mutters through clenched teeth, annoyed at Theo's constant irrelevant remarks.

Zorander flaunts his wicked grin as the iron gate opens once more. But instead of being greeted by demonic monsters, Jake appears with a few dozen female demigods by his side.

'Now this will be fun.' Zorander lets out a deep chuckle as he sits down once more, eager for what is coming next.

'Jake, you don't have to do this,' I plea.

'You wrote your own death wish as soon as you stepped foot onto this island,' he declares.

'I'll rip you, limb from limb,' Alexandros threatens through clenched teeth. Jake responds simply with a smile.

'No way, the hunters of Artemis,' Tia says, finally recognising the girls in front of her. 'Well. I guess your sworn loyalty to Artemis no longer matters,' she adds.

Artemis is the goddess of hunting, vegetation, childbirth, and chastity. She is the twin sister of Apollo. She recruits demigods as her hunters, where they are rewarded with internal youth as long as they serve and remain loyal to her.

They stare at Tia but do not respond.

'I'm confused. You would give up eternal youth, for what? Zorander doesn't care about you, whilst Artemis would do anything for her hunt,' she continues.

'We fight for Zorander!' the girls say in unison, as if in a trance.

Jake adds, 'I've never liked you. I was constantly bored being with you guys. Thinking how powerful you are because, what? You are the children of the big three? Let us see how powerful yo—'

A rock slab from the earth's surface knocks Jake over midsentence.

'I've been wanting to do that for a long time!' Alexandros shouts, standing there amused.

'HA! Good one!' Theo compliments.

Jake wobbles as he gets back up, nostrils flaring.

In unison, the hunters raises their spears to the sky, receiving a wild applause from the audience.

I respond to their war stance by twirling my hands around, a slow circular but efficient motion. I feel the wind circle around me. I summon the air as it attacks them by dislodging their spears from their clenched hands and knocking most of them off their feet.

A few of the still-standing hunters charge towards me. As the first one reaches me, she grabs the swallow that was on her back, a metal handle in the middle that connects the two blades at either end.

Her swallow held upright; she goes for a fore swing followed with a backswing. I dodge, hitting her blade with my own sword.

I make eye contact with her, and for a brief moment, I can see the uncertainty in her eyes. I quickly move to the left and plunge my sword into her.

Before I can breathe, more hunters replace their fallen comrade. Tia and the others join in the fight.

One of the hunter's swings left, right, left. I lunge to the side, dodging her first strikes. Rolling to my left, I raise my sword and block them.

I swing at her, missing as she dodges me, sidestepping, swinging her sword into the side of my armour. It ate through into my thigh, slicing, leaving an open flesh wound.

I fall, my knee dropping. I try to stand up again, but my knee gives way.

'Stop!' Luke yells at the top of his lungs. I can feel the tension in his voice and the intensity in this tone.

Amazingly, everyone stops fighting!

Tia quickly rips some fabric from her shirt, handing it to me. 'Tighten this around your thigh, it will stop the bleeding.'

'We are all family here, children of the Olympian gods! We shouldn't be fighting against each other.' Luke stops, looking at me before continuing on. 'Families can be dysfunctional, but at the end of the day, they will be there for you. We all have darkness, and what makes us who we really are is how we decide to act on it,' Luke says, addressing everyone in the arena. 'Don't fight against us. Stand with us. Fight for what's right. Fight for your home, your family . . . and your freedom.'

Chatter erupts around the arena as demigods reconsider their decisions. This causes Zorander to grow infuriated.

Jake charges towards us, catching us all off guard, straight towards Tia, but just before he reaches her, Luke manages to push Tia to the side, taking the full impact of Jake's blade.

Luke turns, taking one last glance towards me, tears running down his face. The light in his eyes fade, as he drops to the ground, his body *lifeless*.

CHAPTER 37

Last Battle

My eyes widen with horror, my mouth rigid and open. The scream tears through me like a shard of glass. My eyes widen and my heart shudders in my chest as my pulse quickens immensely. The scream comes out again, blood drains from my face. Before I was aware of making any decisions, my legs run furiously towards his lifeless body.

'LUKE!' I drop to his side, his eyes open but empty.

'The sibyl . . .,' Tia chokes. 'She was right.'

'COWARD!' I cry out. 'What did you do?' I shout. I let him down. I promised that I would protect him. I failed.

'Too bad, your speech couldn't save you.' Jake laughs at Luke's lifeless body.

My soul has unleashed a demon—all I feel is anger.

With my fist balled, I hit him, right on his cheekbone. His head flies backwards as he stumbles over, wincing in pain.

'This is between Jake and I,' I let out. 'You just crossed paths with the daughter of Zeus.'

Our swords gleam in the sunlight. I'm going to go up against the very person who took me under his wing and trained me. My mind flashes back briefly to that summer day in Greece, when I wanted nothing more than to be taught how to sword fight. The very same man who trained me killed my only brother in cold blood. He was no longer the sweet guy we all met at the weapons shed. That person is now dead to me, replaced by a traitor and a murderer. I knew that only one of us would walk away from this. His sword still had the blood from his last victim.

Jake charges towards me, letting out a cry. I dodge to the side in one swift move. His eyes dark, he was truly too far gone.

He thrusts his sword forward, only to be met by my sword. They meet in the air with a loud clash. We slash at each other, to which we each defended. Jake was a master swordsman, and this battle was not going to be easily won. However, it looked like he was beginning to get frustrated as he couldn't pass my defenses.

Jake launches forward, both hands on his sword, for *one* last deadly strike. I parry his sword, and in the same movement, I'm able to fling it out of his grasp, and it goes flying through the air. In the same motion, I bring my sword down and thrust it forward, right into his heart. He begins to cough up blood as he chokes, his eyes cover over with gloss, as he falls to the ground with a thud.

'I'm sorry,' I whisper before turning to the others.

The pain that was burning within me began to fade, replaced by numbness. My vision began to blur with the realisation of what I had just done. The only thing I could hear was my own heartbeat. I had killed him.

'Iris . . . Iris!' I am shaken back to reality. Alexandros was standing in front of me, concern written all over his face. 'Are you okay?' he asks.

What a stupid question, I thought to myself. But all I could manage was a simple nod.

He wraps an arm around my shoulders, pulling me close. Despite the emptiness in my stomach, it flutters at the simple gesture.

The crowd of demigods start to shift uncomfortably as they witness many of their own being slaughtered.

Zorander stares in blankness as he cannot comprehend the reality of what has just happened.

He scans the crowd before commanding them, 'WHAT ARE YOU WAITING FOR? ATTACK THEM!'

'You don't have to do this!' I shout in response.

'FIGHT!' Zorander demands.

Many reconsiders their odds and flee to the nearest exit after they had just witnessed us vanquish Zorander's monsters and strongest demigods, leaving only a fraction of loyal followers by Zorander's side.

'Now that evens our odds!' I say.

The remaining demigods then make their way down to the pits, facing directly opposite us.

'The last battle begins!' I shout. 'This war will go down in history, so let us make a difference!'

Alexandros once again summons the undead army. Ready for combat, they emerge from the ground.

Theo summons fire, shooting them towards the demigods that are running towards us, thus keeping them at bay.

I hear a melodious cry, a giant bird fly's over the battlefield, it's feathers beautiful hues of red, yellow, and purple—a phoenix. *(A phoenix can live up to a thousand years before it dies. However, this magical creature will regenerate after death, reborn from its ashes, beginning its next life again.)*

The bird swoops, using its powerful talons, taking out a handful of demigods.

'It's fighting with us!' Tia exclaims.

The clang of our swords fade away. The shouting becomes hushed. As I focus my attention towards Zorander, he was just standing behind his followers, pointing and sending them unknowingly to their deaths.

I make my way towards him, fending off any demigod that makes their way towards me.

Zorander finally notices me, his face turning into a grin, staring me down.

'Scared, Zorander?' I yell towards him. 'Your minions are failing!'

He now stands opposite me as I notice him holding a huge mace. It was a metal shaft with iron spikes protruding from the end.

In that frozen moment, our faces, unreadable. No fear, no cocky smirks.

A string of curses unraveled from his mouth as he advances towards me.

He unleashes a mighty swing, and I roll to the ground to avoid getting struck, then rolling to one side as he smashes the ground, just missing me. I quickly get up, standing my ground.

I thrust my sword towards him, but he blocks my attack, and being the turd that he is, knowingly kicks at my wounded thigh. I let out a cry, wincing at the pain.

Zorander smiles, enjoying the moment.

Breathing in, I steady myself. 'Is that all you got?' I ask, tightening my grip around the handle of my sword.

'Just the beginning.' He chuckles, swinging his mace towards me again, sidestepping. I swing my sword, grazing his arm.

He stops, looks at his arm, wiping the blood dripping from his arm across his forehead. He looks out across the battlefield. The tide has turned. We are winning the battle.

This infuriates Zorander. He looks me dead in the eye, golden light erupting from within him, releasing such an immense force that knocks everyone to the ground.

As I get back up, I notice him beginning to grow. Growing into what? 'Zeus, I'm going to really need your luck now,' I mumble to myself, witnessing Zorander turning into his true form—an all-powerful Titan!

'Not what you expected?' he bellows in a loud voice, rumbling the structure of the arena.

His skin looks like dry dirt. The only part that still confirmed that it was Zorander was his eyes; dark and murderous.

Up above, the sky floods with clouds, pouring us into almost darkness.

I look around to see all my friend's unconscious on the ground, fearing they may not wake up again.

I levitate upwards as power fills within me. For a split second, I think back to the cyclops. This better not *fizzle* out. Lightning shoots from my hands directly towards my evil foe Zorander.

Zorander grins. He had created a shield around himself just before impact, absorbing my lightning. I continue to shoot the lightning bolts towards him. Each time on impact, Zorander lets out an evil laugh.

My hope begins to fade. Luke died for nothing. What am I thinking? *I am* the daughter of the mighty Zeus!

Anger rages through me as I feel the presence of Zeus. Looking up into the thundering dark sky that is spitting out lightning and heavy rain, I yell, 'For Zeus and the gods of Olympus!'

I simultaneously unleash massive thunderbolts from my hands and also from the dark clouds above, thus dramatically intensifying my power. As this new wave hits Zorander's force field, I see cracks beginning to form.

I look at Zorander, and for the first time, I see fear in his eyes as his shield begins to collapse under the immense power, leaving him unprotected. My now uninterrupted full force of rage lightning hits him, and he explodes into a million tiny pieces.

As I stare at the now-empty space that the Titan once stood, Zorander's burnt chunks of flesh fall from the heavens, littering the battlefield. My eyes were still in awe as I realise what I just accomplished. I defeated Zorander. The murderous Titan is now gone.

'Get off me, you retched demigod.' I turn to see that Alexandros had woken up. He shoves an unconscious demigod off his chest. As if suddenly remembering where he was, he jumps up with dagger in hand, turning frantically around, confusion on his face as he takes in his surroundings, realising that I was the only one still standing.

'What's all this cr*p all over me?' he asks, raising an eyebrow. 'What . . . happened?'

Before I answer, I hear Tia grunt as she sits herself up, brushing off all the guts. Theo wakes and as he tries to stand, slips headfirst into the goo. 'EWWW!'

In unison, they ask, 'Why does it smell like a BBQ? And where is Zorander?'

'Dammit!' I yell in frustration. 'You're standing in him. He's in your hair. He's *everywhere!*'

'Say what?' they say, confused.

I respond, 'You won't believe me even if I told you.'

CHAPTER 38

Amends

The silent battlefield comes back to life as demigods begin to stir, realising that we are the ones who defeated their master. They reluctantly side with us, realising the error they had made following Zorander.

Tia and Theo make their way around the battlefield, attending to the wounded in the best of their ability.

Even in the middle of all the chaos, we stayed strong. We are heroes, who vanquished an evil foe, saved Olympus from destruction, and released hundreds of demigods from their false prophet.

The sun began to set off in the horizon. We had survived. We have completed our quest.

Relying on one another's abilities and strength as a united team, led us to this moment's victory.

I stare dazed into the distance; this was all over. The pain in my thigh rushes back as the adrenaline I had during the fight subsided. The wound was throbbing, deep, and painful. I stand there holding my breath, breathing slowly, submerging the panic and pain. I could just waltz right over to Theo, but he had others to heal, ones with much worse injuries than mine.

I tighten the bandage around my thigh, leaving my hands crimson and sticky.

'I found him,' I turn to see Alexandros walking towards me, holding the lifeless body of Luke in his arms.

'Luke,' I whimper.

My hands are shaking so badly as I slowly move towards him, Alexandros places him softly on the ground.

I fall beside him, cradling him in my arms. 'I'm so sorry,' I choke out.

I press my forehead against his as tears begin to burst out, spilling down my face.

Sounding like a distressed child, I feel a comforting hand on my shoulder. I look up, blinking away the tears. The figures slowly form out of the blur. Theo, Tia, and Alexandros stare down at me, their eyes puffy and red.

'It's my fault!' Tia says as she leans down beside Luke.

'It's not your fault . . .,' I respond.

'It is, the Sibyl warned me about this,' she manages to let out.

'Sibyl?' asks Alexandros for me.

'I – I should have mentioned this earlier, but... I didn't believe it. I. I was told that I would be the cause of someone's... death,' she says, avoiding eye contact.

My eyes widen with horror. I don't know if I should lash out or keep silent. 'What do you mean?'

'I'm so sorry,' she apologises again.

'There was nothing we could have done to prevent this outcome. We didn't know that Luke was going to jump in front of you,' Theo tries to comfort Tia.

I cannot be mad at her. Luke wouldn't have wanted that; he saved her life. That's how he should be remembered—as a *hero*.

'I will forever be grateful for him,' Tia says, leaning in and kissing him on his forehead, her eyes cover over with tears.

Alexandros kneels beside me, placing a hand over Luke's heart. 'Theo,' he says, looking up, as if engaged in a secret conversation. 'I've never tried this before. I don't think I have the strength to do it alone.'

'Together?' Theo places his hand over Luke's wound.

'This is far dangerous. We don't know what will happen to Luke or even yourselves,' Tia advises, but they ignore her completely.

Alexandros begins to chant, 'Ζείτε μόνο μία φορά, θυσιάζοντας τη ζωή σας για έναν άλλο. άδης, σας ζητώ να επιστρέψετε την ψυχή του πίσω μας.' *You only live once, sacrificing your life for another. Hades, I ask that you submit his soul back to us.* Grey mist makes its way out of his mouth. His eyes go white as his voice begins to shake the ground all around us.

The supernatural mist that came out of Alexandros surrounds Luke's body, Theo's hands still over the wound as it begins to heal.

This continues for what seems like forever. A crowd of demigods had surrounded us, interested at what is taking place in the middle of the stadium.

Alexandros stops chanting. 'Please let this work, Father,' he pleads, his voice drained, his face looking paler than ever, as if the chant had sucked out a piece of his soul. Suddenly, his eyes roll back, and his body goes limp.

'Alexandros?!' I scream.

Luke's body is now consumed by freezing mist. The mist around him fades, leaving his body alone on the ground.

'What was that supposed to do? Now they're both dead,' the demigods start asking amongst themselves. I stare in shock, hearing whispers.

'That was pointless.'

'Great show.'

The other demigods begin to break rank and walk away.

It feels like I've been staring for an eternity, not knowing what to do. Two of my best friends are now lying *dead* in front of me.

Suddenly, Luke's light-brown eyes snap open, breathing in a breath of air, as he tries to sit up. Still in shock, I cannot believe what is unfolding in front of my eyes.

'Did you miss me?' he says, noticing us all hovering around him.

'Luke?' I say, squeezing him tightly. 'I'm never gonna let you go. Luke, I-I'm so sorry!' I mumble, fresh tears beginning to water my face.

'No more crying!' he says, hugging me back.

Pulling out of the hug, I look around at the others, their mouths open as they stare at Luke alive and well. Now our attention turns to Alexandros, and he slowly begins to stir on the ground. A huge sigh of relief comes over us all.

Luke turns to face Tia. 'Now I think you owe me,' he jokes, giving her a hug.

I turn to Alexandros as he slowly gains consciousness. 'How? You died too!' I ask, motioning towards Luke and himself.

'Being the son of Hades has some perks,' he responds with a whisper and tries to grin, having no strength doing so. 'I won't be trying that again, so no one die on my shift.' It wasn't clear. Did I dream my reaction? Heat rose from my stomach to my chest. I didn't know what took control over me as my lips crashed onto his. Once I've realised what I had just done, I pulled away, blushing, heat rushing to my cheeks as I look away.

'Sorry—'

My apology was cut short as Alexandros pulls me into him, kissing me back. My heart skipping a beat. It was just him and I, it felt as if no one else existed.

'Excuse me!' Luke interrupts, looking down at us. 'I just rose from the dead. Don't take the attention from me.' He chuckles. As if realising where he was, he questions, 'Where's Zorander?'

'He's gone. We don't need to worry about him anymore. Zapped him into oblivion,' I say, smiling. 'That will be a story for another day.'

'And Jake?' Luke spits his name out in disgust.

'He's gone too', Alexandros answers for me. 'Don't worry, I'll keep him *company* in Tartarus,' he says with an evil glint in his eyes.

I turn to address the demigods surrounding us. 'I think it's time to go home.'

The demigods let out cheers of happiness as they hug one another.

One of the younger-looking ginger demigods, about the age of five, makes his way towards me. 'Excuse me, miss?' he says shyly.

'Yes?' I answer, leaning down so that I am eye level with him.

'Would they really accept us? After everything that we have done?' he says with his hands behind his back, rocking back and forth on his heels.

'Yes, definitely! You will be welcomed with open arms,' I say with a huge smile.

The boy runs back into the arms of an older version of himself, his brother.

We lead the *lost* demigods back to the *Argo*, where we sail back towards the sanctuary. No detours this time, straight to Greece.

★☆★

Olympus had summoned us. The gods wished to congratulate the demigods who had saved their kingdom.

'So Zorander was Aetius?' Zeus acknowledges. 'Well, that explains a lot . . .' He rubs his thumb and forefinger over his grey beard, simultaneously thinking centuries back. 'Well done!' he says, turning his attention back toward us, the four prophesised demigods.

We smile amongst ourselves, relieved that the prophecy was now complete.

'Here you thought we wouldn't stand a chance,' Alexandros jabs at his father, trying to receive an outburst from him, but all he received was an impressed look and nod of approval from Hades.

'You did well.' Poseidon sat up in the throne beside Zeus. On the floor beside him was Bear, looking proud as he sat beside the lord of the sea.

Tia smiles back at her father, knowing very well that letting Bear assist, helped us successfully find the *Argo*.

With thanks and a pat on the back, the gods of Olympus sent us off on our way.

I wanted more than anything to inform Aunt Maria and Darius about my adventures, but if I did, I know I'd be on the first taxi back to Monemvasia, never to be able to set foot at the Olympic Sanctuary ever again.

Keeping this from them was the best option. I'm sure they would understand.

CHAPTER 39

Three Months Later

The world requires demigods like us, and maybe one day, we might reveal ourselves to you, and when that day arrives, we hope we are welcomed and not turned away for being peculiar. There is a purpose for our existence—to guard the world from the destruction of monsters and the ones that wish ill of the gods. We truly yearn the freedom of living openly, without having to be deceitful and concealing our true identities. But until that day arrives, be on high alert as you might very well come across a demigod.

The Olympic Sanctuary is thriving more than ever, full of chatter as the 'lost demigods' had made themselves at home, all welcomed openly by the others. Just like the 'Parable of the Prodigal Son,' they realised their mistakes and returned to their family, gifted with a clean slate. Mr. Hargreaves has been treating us like royalty, always going out of his way to make sure we're 'living the best life possible,' which, after some time, does get on our nerves, but he does mean well. We have been gifted the task and responsibility to upskill the demigods at the Olympic Sanctuary, preparing them for any obstacle that may take place. The threatening prophecy we had received, has awaken the demigods at the Sanctuary, as they realise something like this can happen to them at any given moment, without the slightest chance of a warning. But I believe our success with the prophecy has given courage and hope to the demigods, that we managed to defeat an evil fiend, making their lives much simpler without the need to keep an eye out for the 'lost demigods.' Each and every one of the demigods at the Olympic Sanctuary are reaching their full potential as they learn to fight as a team and not against one another. We ensure that they know, every demigod is unique, no matter who their godly parent is, we are all the same in the inside.

Luke has settled in surprisingly well here, the tragic event only happened a few months ago, where I thought I had lost him... He belongs here at the Sanctuary, with me. He has made it his life goal, to show off his skills at every possible moment, fascinating the other children with his ability to change the weather and create thunderstorms whenever he pleased. Our family bond has strengthened, I feel like the prophecy had brought us closer together, I will always be there for him, and I know he will do the same for me.

For the first time in weeks, we have been able to take a step back and relax, to stop and take a long deep breath of fresh air.

'Iris! Come on, it's time for the bonfire,' Alexandros announces as he runs towards me, picking me up with one swift move, twirling me around in the air. 'Put me down!' I giggle. Alexandros holds me gently, cupping my face with one hand, leaning down he kisses me softly. I gaze up at him as butterflies flutter in my stomach. He drew back to study my face for a moment. Smiling lovingly at me, his eyes soft and gentle. For a single moment, time stops. No sanctuary, no demigods, no prophecy, and definitely no gods. It was just him and I.

Oh, I forgot to tell you!

As you have already guessed, Alexandros and I have decided to take things to the next level. I'm sure Zeus isn't too keen on his only daughter dating the son of Hades, but he's not here to tell me otherwise.

We join the others around the campfire, celebrating our victory. Tonight, we swore an oath, a bond that we will take with us to our graves, 'that we will always be there for one another, through thick and thin. No one will be left behind.'

No matter the distance, the space between us, the bond will remain, strong and unbreakable **forever**.

To be continued in the second book of the series.

Trials for the Gods

INDEX

T

V

Z

ABOUT THE BOOK
ILLUSTRATIONS

This book was illustrated by Magic Young, drawn by hand, and finished digitally.

The illustrations in this book were based on the main characters and creatures in the story and inspired by Greek Mythology.

CPSIA information can be obtained
at www.ICGtesting.com
Printed in the USA
FSHW010525080721
83058FS